Forget frustrated. She was desperate.

And there was only one way to ease her torment. Nikki stared at the key card the stranger had pressed into her hand, and the implications rushed through her brain.

Pleasure, pure and simple. Nothing less, but nothing more. This was strictly a barter—sex for sex.

And for the first time in Nikki's life, that didn't seem like such a bad thing. Fighting down a wave of nerves, she knocked on the door.

He answered wearing nothing but a knowing expression. He'd been waiting for her.

She had half a mind to turn and walk the other way. The cowboy looked too certain, with his molten silver eyes and sensuous mouth. His chest was hard and muscular, with dark wisps of silky hair swirling from nipple to nipple. He had broad shoulders and sinewy arms. The tattoos around his biceps seemed dark and dangerous. Primitive. *Forbidden.*

And Nikki could no more resist him than Eve had been able to resist that apple....

Dear Reader,

I love tall, dark and dangerous vampires as much as I love hot, hunky cowboys. So it was just a matter of time before I finally combined the two! The result? Jake McCann, the hero of my newest novel, *Dead Sexy*.

Jake was once a real cowboy before he was forever changed into a lean, mean vamping machine. Now he's a creature of the night who feeds off not only blood, but sex. Lots of sex. Which means that Jake needs a woman. But not just any ordinary filly will do. Jake needs a gal who's bubbling with lust. A female who's overflowing with need. Enter Nikki Braxton, aka Most Likely To Die A Good Girl. Nikki has hooked up with one too many losers and has had far too many dead-end relationships. She wants a normal guy for a change. A guy she can take home to meet the folks. One without a closet full of skeletons or a bunch of weird hang-ups.

Obviously, Jake isn't her man. He's more than one hundred years old and he does have a past. And a few eccentric tastes, if you know what I mean.

I hope you like my first vampire cowboy! I would love to hear your thoughts. You can visit me online at www.kimberlyraye.com or write to me c/o Harlequin Books, 225 Duncan Mill Road, Don Mills, Ontario M3B 3K9, Canada.

Welcome to Skull Creek, Texas! Sit back, enjoy and y'all come back now, ya hear!

Kimberly Raye

KIMBERLY RAYE
Dead Sexy

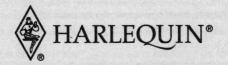

HARLEQUIN®

TORONTO • NEW YORK • LONDON
AMSTERDAM • PARIS • SYDNEY • HAMBURG
STOCKHOLM • ATHENS • TOKYO • MILAN • MADRID
PRAGUE • WARSAW • BUDAPEST • AUCKLAND

ISBN-13: 978-0-373-79362-4
ISBN-10:   0-373-79362-6

DEAD SEXY

www.eHarlequin.com

Printed in U.S.A.

ABOUT THE AUTHOR

USA TODAY bestselling author Kimberly Raye has always been an incurable romantic. While she enjoys reading all types of fiction, her favorites, the books that touch her soul, are romance novels. From sexy to thrilling, sweet to humorous, she likes them all. But what she really loves is writing romance—the hotter the better! She started her first novel back in high school and has been writing ever since. Kim lives deep in the heart of the Texas Hill Country with her very own cowboy, Curt, and their young children. She's an avid reader (she reads *all* the Harlequin Blaze books) who loves Diet Dr. Pepper, chocolate, Toby Keith, chocolate, alpha males—*especially* vampires—and chocolate. Kim also loves to hear from readers. You can visit her online at www.kimberlyraye.com or at www.myspace.com/kimberlyrayebooks.

Books by Kimberly Raye

HARLEQUIN BLAZE

This book is dedicated to cowboys the world over
and the women who love them!

1

HE NEEDED A WOMAN.

If Jake McCann had been anywhere else in the free world, he would have headed for the nearest singles bar. But he was stuck in the middle of nowhere—aka Skull Creek, Texas—and so he'd headed for its one and only pickup spot: the forty-second annual Founder's Day festival, a weeklong celebration that kicked off with tonight's carnival.

He tipped back the brim of his Stetson and studied his surroundings. The rides had been set up on the ten-acre stretch of gravel parking lot behind the local high school. Pastureland surrounded the area, stretching endlessly in all directions, reminding Jake exactly how far out of his element he really was.

No blinding lights or slabs of concrete. No sirens wailing in the distance or horns honking. Instead he heard the whir of rides, barks of laughter and the cry of a violin from the country two-step that drifted from the large tent at the rear of the carnival, where a battle of the local bands had commenced.

There was a giant Ferris wheel and a brightly lit merry-go-round, along with a few more daring rides. Mad Teacups.

The Whirligig. The Octopus. Booths lined the main strip, offering everything from the chance to knock down a dozen milk cans and win a giant stuffed SpongeBob, to hoop shots for a dollar.

He shifted his attention to the two brunettes who stood munching hot dogs near the ringtoss. His gaze locked with one of them and hunger brightened her eyes. She licked her lips suggestively and lust echoed through him. His gaze caught and held number two, who eyed him with the same blatant interest. Her wedding ring winked as she lifted the hot dog to her lips, and he turned away.

His gaze slid to a pretty blonde who clasped the hand of a young boy and dragged him after her. Her brother. Jake knew it even though he didn't know her.

He could see into her thoughts, taste the frustration in her mouth, feel the displeasure that prickled her skin. She'd been stuck babysitting and she wasn't at all happy about it. She'd wanted to hang with her boyfriend tonight. She'd wanted to…

Jake shook away the thought and hopped off that horse before it could run away with him. He was wired enough on his own without letting someone else's fantasies feed the desire already gripping him tight.

He spotted another woman. A knockout in her late thirties. Married. Mentally counting the seconds until she could slip away from her husband and rendezvous with his brother over by the Haunted House. They'd been seeing each other off and on for the past three years. He'd become an addiction she couldn't do without.

Jake knew the feeling.

He had his own addiction.

His own curse.

Not for long.

He'd searched and watched and waited for the past ten years since discovering the means to free himself, and the time had finally come. In nine days he would escape the hunger that held him captive. He would face his past, his sire, and he would defeat him—and then he would be normal again.

A man rather than a vampire.

If he intended to be victorious, he had to be at the top of his game.

Fully alert.

Physically strong.

Emotionally ready.

Powerful.

And there was only one surefire way to beef up his strength—he needed to feed.

Not in the traditional sense. There were some perks to being over one hundred years old—namely he could go days without sinking his fangs into a sweet, succulent female. Contrary to popular myth, the need for blood didn't define him. It was just a part of who he was.

He was also a giant mass of energy.

Tonight's hunt was all about charging that energy. About finding another life force, preferably while it was at its most vibrant, and soaking up the extra voltage.

Tonight's hunt was all about S-E-X.

That's why Jake had left Houston and his motorcycle design business to head for the hill country. He wanted plenty of time to prepare for the coming confrontation. He'd ridden into town just a few hours ago, over a week before his sire was due to return to Skull Creek to relive the turning.

It was what all vampires did on the anniversary of their change. On the exact date, at the exact moment, each was instinctively called back to the site where he or she had left their humanity behind. While reliving the moment of death, a vampire was at his most vulnerable.

Jake had managed to pinpoint the location and he intended to launch his attack while his sire was at his weakest. But he wasn't going to rely on timing alone to guarantee victory.

He'd checked himself into the nearest motel and wasted zero time in heading straight for the one event that offered the biggest selection of females—the carnival that kicked off a weeklong celebration honoring the town's founders. In particular, Sam Black who'd single-handedly fought off a group of Santa Anna's men during the Texas Revolution and preserved the small settlement of Skull Creek.

The man was a legend. A hero.

To everyone but Jake.

He walked toward the ticket booth, looking, sensing, *feeling.* It was another perk of being what he was and the only one he was truly going to miss. Trust had never been a high commodity with the people in his life. Not during the thirty years he'd been human nor in the hundred-plus years since.

Luckily he didn't walk into any situation blindly. He could look into any human's eyes and see their darkest fear, their fondest dream, their deepest desire, their true character. It had saved his ass more than once since he'd been turned and it also kept him from hooking up with the wrong type of woman.

Namely the nice kind. The ones interested in more than a night of hot, wild, steamy sex. The sort who wanted love and marriage and commitment.

All three were impossible for him.

Love? Hell, he'd never been in love with anyone, not when he'd been just a man, and certainly not since he'd turned. He wasn't even sure such a thing existed.

And marriage? Immortality sort of put a crimp in the whole till-death-do-us-part deal.

As for commitment… He had that one down pat, but it didn't involve a female. His dedication centered solely on finding and destroying the vampire who'd turned him back in 1883 and freeing himself once and for all.

Jake's only real potential when it came to the opposite sex involved lots of bone-melting orgasms. That much he could and would guarantee every woman. Rather than deceive anyone, he preferred to be as up-front as possible. Obviously he wasn't anxious to get himself staked, so he kept the vampire part to himself. But his intentions—sex and nothing but sex—he made crystal clear.

Satisfaction.

That was the only promise Jake ever made.

The only one he could keep.

He kept walking, his boots crunching gravel with each step. The cool evening breeze slid over his bare arms and whispered over his skin, feeding the anxiety already gripping him tight. His gaze slid this way and that.

Just beyond the roar of the rides and the squeals of laughter, he heard the sharp intake of breath. A soft gasp that popped in his head and stoked the fire in his blood.

The sound drew him around the corner, away from the games, toward the food section which had been separated into three aisles: Sweets Boulevard, Vegetable Drive and Hearty Meat Street.

He turned down the first aisle and stopped a few feet shy of one booth draped in vibrant pink tulle. His gaze zeroed in on the woman who waited for a mountain of cotton candy to be draped around a white paper cone.

Her long strawberry-blond hair had been pulled back into a simple ponytail. She wore jeans and a T-shirt, the name *Dog the Bounty Hunter* emblazoned across the back.

She wasn't the most beautiful woman he'd ever seen. But there was just something about her…a warmth that sizzled through the air between them and drew his undivided attention.

"Thanks, Molly," she told the forty-something woman who handed her the treat. She fished in her pocket for a dollar bill.

"On the house," Molly told her, waving the money away. "Just make sure you squeeze me in for a color tomorrow afternoon. I want to look my best for the rib cook-off tomorrow night." She grinned. "I think Arliss Dupree is going to ask me out. I heard from Mabel who heard from Louise who heard from Denise Duttmeyer that he was seen stocking up on antacids." A dreamy look crept into the older woman's eyes. "I just love a man who plans ahead."

"Call the salon first thing in the morning and I'll work

you in." She stuffed the money back into her pocket and started to turn.

"And, by the way, just you never mind about Bill." The cotton candy lady waved her hand. "He's a slimy turd and you're better off without him."

The blonde stiffened, and even though Jake couldn't see her face, he felt the disappointment that rolled through her. And the embarrassment.

"And here I always thought he was such a nice boy," Molly went on. "Just goes to show that you can't trust anybody, even a savings-and-loan officer. If he'll lie about going to Vegas on the pretense of attending a seminar only to have an orgy with a couple of strippers, he'll fudge on interest rates, that's for damn sure."

"I… It's okay, really. It's not like we were engaged or anything." *Not yet.*

The silent thought crossed the distance to Jake and echoed in his head. Anger rolled through him and his fingers tightened. He had the sudden urge to hunt down the slimy turd and beat him to a bloody pulp.

"If you need anything," Molly told her, "you know where to find me. Or if you want my nephew Zeke to break his ankles, I can arrange that, too. Zeke always liked you, you know."

"Really? I never would have guessed, what with the way he ran over my lunch with his bike back in the sixth grade."

"Aw, honey, my poor, departed Reggie—God rest his soul—did the same thing to me back when we were in grade school." Molly beamed. "Men just have their own way of expressing themselves. Haven't you read that Mars and Venus book? You really ought to read that. You might have better luck with the fellas."

"Thanks." *Not*. The thought slid across the distance to him as clear and distinct as if she'd whispered directly in his ear. "I'll keep my eye out for it." She turned then, giving him his first real look at her face.

His heart paused and he stopped breathing for a long, drawn-out moment. Not that he needed oxygen, mind you, but old habits really were hard to break. And this particular one made it easier to blend in and preserve his anonymity.

His pulse quickened as his gaze roved over her.

She wasn't exceptionally beautiful. She wore very little makeup and her mouth wasn't as full as he usually liked. But there was an excitement that burned in her whiskey-colored eyes as she stared at the candy confection in her hand. A vibrancy that zipped down his spine and fireballed smack-dab in his gut. All thoughts of revenge faded into a rush of need that drew his body painfully tight.

He watched as she touched the fluffy sweet to her lips and felt the satisfaction that pulsed hot and consuming at the first luscious bite. She closed her eyes, letting the candy melt on her tongue, but the taste lasted only a few blissful seconds and did little to relieve the anxiety knotting her muscles.

Because she didn't really want cotton candy. Or funnel cakes. Or caramel apples. Or any of the other treats being dished up at the various booths that lined the aisle.

She wanted something richer—and much more potent.

She stiffened and two tiny lines pinched between her eyebrows. A subtle change that no one else seemed to notice. Hell, other than the occasional hello from a friendly face, no one really noticed her at all.

Except for Jake.

He saw the disappointment that clouded her gaze and the stiff way she held her shoulders and he felt the rest—the hot rush of blood through her veins, the frantic beat of her heart, the buzz of her nerves and the tingle of her nipples.

She was a bubbling cauldron of repressed sexual energy just waiting to boil over.

Jake smiled and stepped forward.

It was time to turn up the heat.

2

NIKKI BRAXTON WAS through with men and relationships.

Done.

Finished.

That's all, folks!

She eyed the mountain of whispery pink sugar and smiled. From here on out, she was eating her way to happiness.

She lapped at the sweetness and focused on the rush of happy that surged from her brain to the tips of her toes and back up again. Sugar was definitely the way to go.

That's what she told herself as she snagged a piece of cotton candy with her finger and popped it into her mouth. Her taste buds tingled and her frustration eased. Temporarily, of course.

But then, that was the story of her life.

Another bite, another surge of satisfaction, and she started to think that maybe, just maybe, the phone call from Bill two weeks ago, complete with a very graphic, albeit accidental, image from his picture phone, had been a good thing.

Okay, it hadn't been so great that he'd purposely sent the pic to his bowling buddies, who, in turn, had shown everyone and their dog. Which meant the entire town had shared in her humiliation.

Even so, it wasn't the end of the world.

So what if Bill—the two-timing jerk—had cheated on her? So what if he was still in Vegas, holed up with two pairs of fake boobies, having a bona fide orgy, just as Molly had said? Good riddance. He'd been a mama's boy who still lived at home, and she'd wasted seven months on him already. Seven months of Friday-night dinners with him and his mother and Saturday-night movie dates with him and his mother and Sunday picnics with him and—you guessed it—his mother.

While seven didn't sound like a lot, add it to the sixteen months she'd wasted with Roger Beeville (he'd had a thing for women's shoes that had driven him to swipe every pair during tournament week down at the bowling alley), the thirteen months before that with Stan Caufield (he'd had a thing for his secretary...and his cleaning lady, and the clerk down at the video store and the acrylic-nail girl at Nancy's Nails) and the eighteen months before that with Jerry Whatshisname (he'd had a thing for his old football buddy named Buck), and it amounted to a lot of wasted time. Factor in at least six months between each for a decent mourning period (and enough Hershey's Kisses to dull the pain), and we were talking *years*.

Forget the optimistic twenty-two-year-old she'd been with a brand-spanking-new degree in cosmetology and dreams of her own happily ever after—a nice, reliable man, two kids, a couple of dogs and a house with a huge backyard. She was now thirty years old and the stressed-out owner of her own hair salon, To Dye For. She had a monstrous bank loan and an endless string of bad relationships with dysfunctional men.

She also had a giant mortgage.

While she'd given up on the guy for now, she saw no reason to hinge everything on Mr. Nice and Reliable. Sure, she wasn't ready to go it alone when it came to kids, or even the dogs, but she was more than capable of buying a house and taking at least a small step toward her happily ever after.

She'd done so last week and had spent every night since making a list of needed repairs—they didn't call it a fixer-upper for nothing. She still had a lot to do, from painting to new flooring, but she felt good. Productive.

If only she felt *satisfied*.

Instead she was wound tighter than an extrakinky perm. She needed an orgasm in the worst way.

The knowledge stuck in her brain as she turned to walk toward the dunking booth just around the corner.

Not that she couldn't head home right this second and treat herself if she felt like it. She shopped online, like every other woman in her small town, and she had her own personal arsenal of female sex toys. She was more than capable of handling the situation on her own. But she knew from past experience that the release would be all too brief. Even more, there was no satisfaction in snuggling with a multispeed vibrator.

She needed a flesh-and-blood man for that.

Hence Bill.

Seven months of snuggling and cuddling and making out—when they were able to elude his mother, that is—and she'd finally been ready to go all the way. She'd planned a big welcome home at his place, complete with a home-cooked dinner and herself as the dessert. A huge offering for a woman who'd grown up hearing her great-aunt Izzie preach, "A man won't buy the cow if he gets the milk for free."

Old-fashioned. Sexist. The saying was both. And it was also true. Nikki's mother—Izzie's niece—had spent her entire life "giving it away," and not once had she ever had a meaningful, lasting relationship.

There'd been no joint checking account, no mono-grammed towels, no picture perfect family gathered around the Thanksgiving table. There'd been only Aunt Izzie, Nikki, Nikki's mother, and whatever man Nikki had been calling "Uncle" that week.

Nikki had wanted more for herself. A solid, lasting re-lationship. *Permanent.* And so she'd taken Izzie's advice and held back.

Not that she was a virgin, mind you. She'd done the deed a handful of times in the past. With Jerry (before he'd started wearing her underwear). And with Stan (before he'd started wearing her shoes). But with each man she'd waited a decent amount of time. Long enough to preserve her nice-girl status and really get to know him.

Or so she'd thought.

She tugged at another fluff of pink and popped it into her mouth. There. Talk about ecstasy. No batteries needed. No waiting period required. No weird hidden fetish ready to jump up and bite her when she least expected it.

It didn't get much better.

"Wanna bet?" The deep, masculine voice slid into her ears and snagged her out of the sugar high dulling her senses.

Every nerve in Nikki's body snapped to attention as she stopped and turned. Her gaze collided with a pair of eyes so gray and translucent they looked silver.

Excitement pumped through her, followed by a bolt of desire that gripped every inch of her body and stalled the air in her lungs. She forgot to breathe for the next several seconds as she drank in the cowboy who'd come up behind her.

He had a great face. Not the perfect *GQ* kind but a face that said he was every bit as rough and rugged as his voice implied.

Beneath the brim of his black Stetson, his gaze gleamed hot and bright and knowing. Stubble darkened his strong jaw, circled his sensuous mouth and crept down the column of his throat. Dark hair curled from beneath his hat and brushed his collar.

He stood well over six feet, his shoulders broad and massive beneath a black T-shirt. Just below the edge of his sleeves, ornate slave-band tattoos circled each muscular bicep. Faded jeans cupped his crotch, clung to his thighs and traced the outline of his long, sinewy legs. He wore scuffed black cowboy boots and an air of raw sexuality that made her nipples tingle.

Oh, boy.

That was her first cohesive thought when she actually started to breathe again.

Okay, maybe it wasn't her *first* thought.

Number one? *Oh, no.*

She became keenly aware of the raggedy old tee and baggy jeans she'd pulled on prior to leaving the house.

Shapeless. Unattractive. The perfect attire for stripping and painting the walls of her dream house.

For meeting hot guys? It definitely lacked.

Then again, she hadn't come here to meet guys. She'd come to satisfy her sweet tooth.

The reminder was enough to spark some sense, and she forced her lips to move. "Excuse me?" she finally managed.

His grin was slow and easy, wiping away the mesmerizing intensity and replacing it with an irresistible charm that eased the thunder of her heart.

Instead of answering her question, he simply stared at her, into her, for a long moment before he nodded toward the mountain of spun sugar she held in her hand. "Mind if I have a taste?"

It wasn't even close to a decent pickup line, and she couldn't stifle the disappointment that rushed through her.

Obviously this tall, dark and delicious cowboy had fallen head over heels for her cotton candy rather than her.

Just the way Bill had fallen for the strippers and Jerry had fallen for that pair of silver Michael Kors sandals he'd bought for her birthday.

Another guy with a fetish. Great. Just great.

Not that it mattered. She'd sworn off men, and this guy was just more fuel to add to the proverbial fire.

She shrugged. "Sure." She held up the pink treat. "Knock yourself out."

His grin widened and he leaned forward.

And then he kissed her.

3

HIS STRONG, PURPOSEFUL mouth claimed hers. His tongue swept her bottom lip, licking and nibbling and—

Wait a second.

Nikki's heart thundered as she struggled to grasp the current scenario. This was *not* happening. No way was a hot, sexy stranger kissing her for no apparent reason, in front of God and everyone, including the senior ladies' bingo squad. From the corner of her eye Nikki glimpsed a dozen pairs of bifocals trained on her.

On him.

On *them.*

No *friggin'* way.

Just as the denial registered in her shocked brain, he deepened the kiss. His tongue pushed inside and tangled with her own. All rational thought faded in a tsunami of hunger that washed over her, drenched every inch of her body and made her tremble from the sheer force.

He tasted like sweet honey and hot, potent male—and something she couldn't quite name. Something dark and dangerous and mesmerizing.

Before she could stop herself, she melted against him.

Her hands slid up his chest and her fingers caught the soft, dark hair at the nape of his neck.

His arms closed around her. Strong hands pressed against the base of her spine, drawing her closer. She met him chest for chest, hip for hip, until she felt every incredible inch of him flush against her body—the hard planes of his chest, the solid muscles of his thighs, the growing erection beneath his zipper.

Heat spread from her cheeks, creeping south. The slow burn traveled inch by tantalizing inch, until her nipples throbbed and wetness flooded between her thighs, and all because he'd kissed her.

Because she'd kissed him.

Because they were *still* kissing.

Beyond the buzz of desire and the chaos of the carnival, she heard the shocked "Why, I *never.*"

Mumbled agreement echoed among the old women gathered nearby, followed by a "Disgraceful," and a "Hmph, looks like the apple don't fall too far from the tree."

The words registered and she stiffened. Tearing her lips away, she stumbled backward.

Breathe, she told herself. *Just breathe.* "I… We…" She shook her head and tried to make some sense out of everything. "What just happened?"

He eyed her, his gaze hot and bright as he stared down at her. "I kissed you."

"I know that. But *why?* I mean, I thought you wanted a taste of my candy."

"I never said that."

"You implied it."

His gaze darkened as it touched her mouth, and again she felt the overwhelming chemistry that pulsed between them. So hot and powerful that it was almost palpable. "I wanted a taste of you." He licked his own lips. "I still do."

So do I.

She fought down the shameless thought and focused on her outrage rather than the desire fogging her senses. Her spine went ramrod straight. "I don't know who you are or what you're trying to pull, but what you just did was way out of line, buddy."

"Is that so?" His eyebrow arched as if he knew she didn't buy the outburst any more than he did.

"You're lucky I don't call security and have them haul your butt away for accosting me."

"Accosting, huh? Sounds interesting." He grinned and her heart kicked up a notch.

"You can't just walk around kissing strange women."

"I didn't kiss a strange woman. I kissed a woman who kissed me back."

"I didn't mean to… That is, you caught me off guard. I wasn't thinking."

"No, you were following your instincts." He winked. "It's the basic law of attraction."

"I'm not attracted to you."

"Why not?"

Good question. "Because…I'm just not. I don't even know your name. And you don't know mine. We—" she waved her hand back and forth between the two of them "—don't even know each other."

"We could *get* to know each other."

"Are you asking me out?"

"I'm asking you in, sugar. To my hotel room. I'm just passing through and I don't have much time." His grin faded. "I want you and you want me. We should do something about that."

"Well, I...I..." *I never* was right there on the tip of her tongue. But the last thing she wanted was to admit the sad truth out loud. She'd never had anyone make such a proposition.

She'd never wanted one.

Until now.

She shook away the thought. "You're arrogant. And presumptuous."

"And right." He leaned in close, his lips grazing her ear. "You *do* want me."

"Says you."

"Says this." He moved so quickly that she didn't have time to blink, much less anticipate his touch. His fingertips grazed the side of her breast, and her nipple instantly pebbled. Her lips trembled and she swayed ever so slightly. "So let's do something about it."

"Sex," she blurted. "I... This is crazy." She wasn't doing it. She couldn't. "I'm sorry if you got the wrong idea, but I don't... I can't... I mean, I won't. I don't do one-night stands."

He didn't say a word. He just leaned back and stared down at her. Her nipples tingled in response. The pressure started deep, spreading, consuming, until it was all she could do not to lean forward and press herself shamelessly against him.

Talk about a mixed message.

He looked at her for several long seconds, as if he couldn't quite believe she was turning him down. Oddly enough, there was nothing arrogant about his expression. Rather, he seemed genuinely surprised.

Finally he shook his head and reached into his pocket. His warm fingers played at hers as he reached for her hand.

"I'm at the Skull Creek Inn." He pressed a cold piece of plastic into her palm. "If you change your mind."

But she wouldn't, because Nikki Braxton didn't jump into bed with a stranger, no matter how good-looking. She'd spent her entire life playing the good girl, holding back, convinced that by doing so she could guarantee a solid, lasting relationship.

And how's that working for you?

The question haunted her for the next few hours as she gorged herself on funnel cakes, homemade fudge and a huge hunk of Miss Emma's award-winning chocolate cake, and tried to forget the most incredible kiss of her life.

But she couldn't forget, she finally admitted as she climbed behind the wheel of her Ford Explorer. Any more than she could avoid the truth: despite her best efforts, she was no closer to her own happily ever after than her mother had been. Even more, she was sexually frustrated to the point that she'd melted at the booted feet of a virtual stranger. And she'd totally embarrassed herself in front of the ladies' bingo squad.

Her flawless reputation had died in a matter of seconds, and just like that she'd gone from good girl to a chip off the old block.

Forget frustrated. She was desperate.

And there was only one way to ease the anxiety eating up her common sense.

She stared at the key card he'd pressed into her hand, and the implication rushed through her brain.

Pleasure, pure and simple. Nothing less but nothing more.

Her fingers closed around the plastic, and she had the sudden urge to chuck it into the nearest trash can.

No man's going to buy the cow if he can get the milk for free.

But this wasn't about making a purchase.

This was strictly a barter. Sex for sex. Temporary.

For the first time in Nikki's life that didn't seem like such a bad thing.

She keyed the ignition, gunned the engine and pulled out of the high school parking lot. Five minutes later, she pulled up next to a shiny black-and-chrome chopper parked behind Skull Creek's one and only motel.

Fighting down a wave of nerves, she walked to the door and knocked.

He answered wearing nothing but a pair of blue jeans and a knowing expression that said he'd had no doubt that she would show up.

He'd been waiting for her.

She had half a mind to turn and walk the other way. He looked too certain with his molten silver eyes and sensuous mouth. Too handsome. His chest was hard and muscular. Dark wisps of silky hair swirled from nipple to nipple. He had broad shoulders and sinewy arms. The ornate tattoos around his biceps made him seem darker and more dangerous. Primitive. *Forbidden.*

And she could no more resist him than Eve had been able to resist that ripe, juicy apple.

"Nikki Braxton," she blurted. "Thirty years old. I own the local beauty salon. Born and raised right here in town. I like the Pussycat Dolls, chocolate pudding and playing solitaire on my computer. And I'm forever in search of new highlight colors."

And then *she* kissed *him*.

4

THE MOMENT NIKKI touched her lips to his, Jake felt a wave of heat unlike anything he'd ever felt before. Her lips were so warm, so hungry, so damned different from any female he'd ever been with.

He was always the aggressor.

The predator.

Not this time. She backed him up into the hotel room and kicked the door shut with her foot. Her tongue tangled with his and she slid her arms around his neck. Her small fingers splayed in his hair, and heat shimmered down his spine from the point of contact.

His gut clenched and his body throbbed and suddenly he was back in the driver's seat. He slid his arms around her waist, shoved his hands beneath her T-shirt and felt her bare skin. She was soft and warm and his body trembled. He steered her around toward the bed and urged her down. He pulled back, his hands going to the button on his jeans. He made quick work of them, shoving the denim down his legs so fast that it was a wonder he didn't fall flat on his ass.

Her gaze fell to his massive erection and she hesitated. She was having second thoughts, damning herself for being so impulsive.

Jake fought for his control and steeled himself against the delicious heat coming off her body. Because he didn't just want to take from her. He wanted her to give.

The notion stuck. A crazy, insane notion, but he couldn't help himself. He'd spent a century taking, drinking, feeding, and for once he wanted to know what it felt like for a woman to give herself. Not because he demanded but because she wanted to.

He closed his hands over her shoulders, guiding her down onto the mattress. His fingers skittered over the soft material of her T-shirt, molding the cotton to her full breasts.

Easy…

The warning sounded in his head, and he managed to move his hands away before he could stroke her perfectly outlined nipples.

He scooted down to pull off her sneakers and toss them to the floor. Then his fingers went to the button on her jeans. His heart pounded and his pulse raced and an ache gripped him from the inside out. He stiffened, fighting the urge that roared inside of him.

Slow…

He smoothed the denim down her legs. His fingertips brushed her bare skin, grazing and stirring. The friction ripped through him, testing his control with each delicious inch. Finally, *finally,* he stood near the foot of the bed and pulled the jeans free of her long legs.

Clad only in the thin cotton shirt and lace panties, she looked so damned sweet and innocent. So opposite of any of the women he usually kept company with. He grew harder, hotter, and anticipation zipped up and down his spine.

His gaze traveled from her calves, up her lush thighs, to the wispy lace barely covering the soft strip of blond silk between her legs.

He swallowed, his mouth suddenly dry. With a sweep of his tongue he licked his lips. The urge to feel her pressed against his mouth nearly sent him over the edge. He wanted to part her with his tongue and taste all of her secrets. Need pounded, steady, demanding, and sent the blood jolting through his veins at an alarming rate.

The hunger roared inside of him and made him think crazy-ass thoughts. Like how she was just about the most beautiful woman he'd ever seen and how he wanted her more than any other woman in his past.

Because she was different from every woman.

He stared deep into her eyes. Gone was the glimmer of loneliness he'd glimpsed earlier. He saw only uncertainty now. And anticipation.

His hands started to tremble and he felt a driving force wrap around him, propel him toward her. He dropped to the bed beside her and reached out. His fingers brushed the velvet of one hip.

It wasn't enough.

His hands seemed to move of their own accord, traveling the length of her body, exploring every curve, every dip, lingering at the lace covering her moist heat.

He traced the pattern with his fingertip, moving lower until he could feel the slit between her legs. She gasped and her legs opened. She wanted more and he wanted to give it to her. He followed the edge of her panties and barely resisted the need to dip his fingers beneath and plunge one deep into her lush body.

Not yet. She was still too stiff. Too wary. Despite the growing desire that flushed her skin a bright, delicious pink.

Jake tamped down on his hunger and forced his hand up over her flat belly. Her soft flesh quivered beneath his palm as he moved higher, pushing her T-shirt up until he uncovered one creamy breast.

His fingertips circled the rose-colored nipple, and he inhaled sharply when the already turgid peak ripened even more.

Leaning over, he touched his lips to her navel, dipped his tongue inside and swirled. She whimpered, the sound urging him on. He licked a path up her fragrant skin, teasing and nibbling, until he reached one full breast. Closing his lips over her swollen nipple, he pulled and tugged.

He swept his hands downward, cupping her heat through the scanty lace of her panties. Wisps of silky hair brushed his palm like licks of fire, stoking the hunger that already raged inside of him.

She gasped and arched toward him. But despite her reaction, there was something inside of her that still held back.

"Jake McCann," he murmured, his lips grazing her nipple. "I was born and raised in a hole-in-the-wall town called Junction. My favorite color is blue and I like horses."

THE DEEP HUSKY VOICE echoed in Nikki's ears, and she opened her eyes to stare up at the man leaning over. His hand stilled between her legs, his palm pressed tightly to her sex.

"C-can you ride?" She wasn't sure how she managed the question. The heat from his touch seeped into her, making her head spin. But she managed anyway, her curiosity getting the best of her.

His gaze glittered hot and bright, like liquid silver. "Darlin', I can ride better than I can walk."

He hooked one finger under the edge of her panties and pushed the lace to the side. He trailed his fingertips over her moist flesh, his gaze never leaving hers. As if he knew how wound up she was. As if he knew his effect on her.

He knew her.

Inside and out.

She stiffened at the unsettling thought. But then he pushed a finger deep inside and she stopped thinking altogether.

She gasped, her lips parting, her eyes drifting closed at the intimate caress.

"Open your eyes," Jake demanded, his voice raw with savage lust. "I want to look at you. I want to see what's in your eyes when you come apart for me."

Nikki obeyed and he caught her gaze. He slipped another finger inside her.

Her legs turned to butter. Her knees fell open, giving him better access.

But he didn't go deeper and give her more of what she wanted. Instead he stared down at her, his gaze so compelling that she couldn't help herself. She arched her hips, rising up to meet him, drawing him in.

The more she moved, the deeper he went. The pressure built.

"That's it, sugar. You're getting closer."

She continued to move from side to side, creating the most delicious friction, her insides slick, sweltering from his invasion. She tried to breathe, to pull oxygen into her lungs, but she couldn't seem to get enough. Pleasure rippled from her head to her toes, and the room seemed to spin around her. Her hips rotated. Her nerves buzzed.

She hadn't felt so good in a long, long time.

If ever.

She ignored the outrageous thought and concentrated on the feelings roiling inside of her. Her head fell back. Her lips parted. A low moan rumbled up her throat and spilled past her lips.

He leaned down and caught the sound with his mouth. His hand fell away from her as he thrust his tongue deep, mimicking the careful attention his purposeful fingers had given her only seconds before.

Straddling her, his knees trapped her thighs. He leaned back to gaze down at her. He was a black silhouette, a man made of shadows, a *stranger*.

She knew his name, she reminded herself. And his favorite color. And there was just something about him, an understanding that said he knew her all too well. Her likes. Her dislikes. Her fears.

Hello? We're talking a one night stand here. Stop thinking and just feel.

She touched his bare chest, felt the wisps of hair beneath her palm, the ripple of muscle as he sucked in a deep breath. Her attention shifted lower and she grasped him, trailing her hand up and down his shaft. His flesh pulsed in her palm and a shiver danced up her spine. She wanted to feel him. She wanted it more than she'd ever wanted anything.

He thrust into her grip as she worked him for several long moments before he caught her wrist and forced her hand away. He leaned down and snatched his jeans off the floor. ~~Pulling a condom from his pocket, he ripped open the package and rolled the latex down his penis.~~

And then he touched her.

His hands started on her rib cage and slid her T-shirt up and over her head. He touched her anywhere, everywhere, as if he knew what she craved better than he knew himself.

He did.

The truth hit her as she stared into his silver gaze and saw her own ferocious hunger mirrored in the bright depths. He knew her, all right. He knew her frustration. Her need.

He felt them both.

She wondered if he had his own string of fetish-ridden ex-girlfriends. He lowered his head then and drew her nipple into the moist heat of his mouth, and suddenly the only thing on her mind was touching him. She slid her hands over his shoulders, feeling his warm skin and hard muscle.

He suckled her breast, his teeth grazing the soft globes, nipping and biting with just enough pressure to make her gasp. Her breast swelled and throbbed.

Jake licked a path across her skin to coax the other breast in the same torturous manner. A decadent heat spiraled through her and she moved her pelvis. She wanted him, surrounding her, inside of her.

"Not yet," he murmured as if he'd read her thoughts. He slid down her slick body and left a blazing path with the velvet tip of his tongue. Strong, purposeful hands parted her thighs. Almost reverently, he stroked her quivering sex.

The breath rushed from her lungs when she felt his damp mouth against the inside of one thigh. Then his lips danced across her skin to the part of her that burned the fiercest.

She gasped as his tongue parted her. He eased his hands under her buttocks, tilting her to fit more firmly against his mouth. His shoulders urged her legs apart until she lay completely open.

He nuzzled her, drinking in her scent before he devoured her with his mouth. Every thrust of his tongue, every caress of his lips, felt like a raw act of possession that branded her *mine, mine, all mine.*

If only.

As soon as the thought pushed its way into her head, she pushed it right back out. There was no hidden meaning behind his actions. It was all about the pursuit of pleasure.

A temporary pleasure.

Regret washed through her, but then his fingers parted her slick folds and his tongue swept her. Up and down. Back and forth.

Heat drenched her. She bucked and her body convulsed. A rush of moisture flooded between her thighs, and he lapped at her as if he'd never tasted anything so sweet.

When she calmed to a slight shudder, he slid up the damp length of her body, gathered her in his arms and kissed her. She tasted her essence—wild and ripe, bitter and sweet—on his lips and desire spurted through her.

She slid her hands over his shoulders and traced the

sinewy contours of his body. His length pulsed between her legs, pressing against her tender flesh.

But he didn't enter her.

Not yet.

Instead he devoured her with his mouth, his hands roaming her body, stroking pleasure points she never knew existed.

"Now," she begged when she could take no more. She arched against him, opening herself up, desperate to pull him deep.

He growled and grasped her hips. Thrusting he joined them in one swift, complete motion.

The air rushed from her lungs, only to rush back in as she gasped.

He pulsed deep inside of her for a long, decadent moment before he started to move. He withdrew, only to push back inside burying himself deep.

Once. Twice.

She skimmed her hands over his back, urging him harder, faster, as she felt the bubbling heat of another climax.

Again?

She couldn't believe how quickly she was ready for round two. Then again, it had been so long since she'd had a round one that it only made sense. It certainly wasn't Jake himself who stirred her until she was desperate and out of control.

She was horny, that's all.

She came quickly. She clutched at his shoulders. She cried out his name.

He buried himself one last time deep in her body and went rigid.

Through the fuzzy haze of pleasure, Nikki glimpsed him

poised above her, his arms braced on either side. His muscles bulged. His skin glistened with perspiration. His eyes were wide-open. His gaze shimmered, pulsing into a hot, vibrant purple that glowed in the darkness. His lips parted, and she caught a flash of white as he bared his teeth—

Wait a second.

She blinked, and there he was still poised above her. But his eyes were closed, the vibrant color just a memory. His brow furrowed. His lips parted, revealing a row of straight, white, *normal* teeth. A groan rumbled from his throat as he gave in to his own orgasm. He stiffened, bucking once, twice, before collapsing atop her.

She felt a rush of panic, but then he gathered her in his arms. His strength surrounded her and eased the sudden tension in her body. He nuzzled her neck, his lips warm against her pulse beat.

She closed her eyes and saw him in her mind's eye. His eyes blazing and his teeth—

Her eyes snapped open. She'd been on the wagon so long that she was hallucinating. She cupped his cheek and felt the warmth of his skin. The faint hint of stubble tickled her palm. Real.

And she wanted more.

The realization hit her, along with a rush of panic. Because she'd never wanted a man so badly.

The wrong man, she reminded herself. Then again, she didn't know him well enough to know one way or the other at this point. Not that she would ever find out. He was temporary. A fantasy come to life.

And suddenly there seemed nothing wrong with pretending that Jake was the right man. The guy who would sweep her off her feet and carry her over the threshold and love her from this day forward, till death do us part.

It's not as if he would ever know.

She slid her arms around his neck and gave in to the incredible urge to kiss him.

To love him.

Until the night ended and they said goodbye.

FORGET SUNLIGHT AND wooden stakes.

Neither posed half as much danger as the woman curled up next to him.

Lush. Blatantly sexual. Insatiable.

She was all three. A dream come true to a vampire who fed off sexual energy. Or she would have been except for the fact that, despite all of the above, she was an innocent.

Not a virgin, mind you.

Jake could spot those the way he sensed any other threat. She'd had her share of sexual encounters, but they'd been few and far between. Deep inside, she was naive when it came to men. Still nursing those pie-in-the-sky dreams of a knight in shining armor and *forever.*

Shit.

Jake eased his arm out from under her. The best thing to do was cut his losses and get the hell out of here right now.

Sure, he'd planned to rejuvenate all night, but the last thing—the very last thing—he needed to do was spend an entire night with Nikki Braxton.

Not because she wanted more from him than he could

give but because for a few crazy seconds he'd actually wanted to give her more.

When she'd slid her arms around his neck and stared deep into his eyes as if he were the love of her life, he'd actually let himself get caught up in the fantasy, as well.

He'd liked having a woman look at him with something other than lust in her eyes. He'd liked it too damned much. So much that he'd forgotten himself for those few seconds and the hunger had reared its ugly head and he'd come this close—this friggin' *close*—to tasting more than just her sex.

Holy shit.

He sat up and threw his legs over the side of the bed. She slept soundly next to him. But he had no illusions that she would stay that way. She would wake just as soon as she regained her strength. Hot and eager for another round.

Her brow furrowed as if she sensed his sudden movement. He touched her forehead and stroked away the worry lines.

Relax. He sent the silent thought and her expression eased.

He reached for the sheet that bunched at the bottom of the bed. He meant to pull it up over her. He really did. But then his gaze snagged on her pink toes and he couldn't help himself. He wanted to look at her.

One last look.

His gaze traveled over delicate ankles, up her calves, her knees, to her hips. The single strip of pubic hair leading to the slit that separated her lush pink lips.

Jealousy burned through him as he thought of someone—male or female—waxing and pampering and touching her so intimately. Truthfully he'd never cared much for all the primping that most women did these days. He'd come from an era where natural was in. Staring at Nikki, however, he had to admit that he sort of liked the look.

He liked everything about her.

Before he could think too much on the subject, he forced his attention up and on, over her soft, smooth stomach to her rose-tipped breasts. He traced the indentation of her clavicle, the smooth column of her throat.

Her strawberry-blond hair fanned out across the pillow. Her nostrils flared, and a soft snore rumbled past her slightly parted lips.

Pull the sheet up, he told himself. *Now.*

Before he could get the cover past her waist, his attention snagged on one dark nipple. His mouth watered as he remembered the tight bud against his tongue. As if he'd actually reached out, the tip grew hard, swelling beneath his eyes. He felt the energy whirling inside of her, the wildness as it stirred and grew.

"Where are you going?" Her soft voice pushed past the thunder of his heart, and his gaze collided with hers.

Rich, golden eyes fringed in long eyelashes stared back at him. He had the fleeting thought that he'd climbed from the bed on purpose.

Get while the getting is good, a voice reminded him.

But then she smiled and touched his throbbing erection, and suddenly the only thing he could think of was how he wanted inside of her again.

5

THE FIRST FIERY FINGERS of dawn threatened the horizon as Jake straddled the black-and-chrome motorcycle parked in front of the Skull Creek Inn and keyed the ignition.

He kicked the bike into gear, and a roar split open the early-morning silence. He gunned the engine and shifted into first. Gravel spewed as he left the parking lot behind and swerved out onto Main Street.

A few seconds later, he hit the county road leading out of town and picked up his speed. The wind whipped at him, but it did little to cool the fire heating him from the inside out. He was wired. Fully charged. His senses more alive than they'd been in a very long time.

Over the buzz of the wind he heard the rustle of a rabbit in the nearby brush, the buzz of the crickets, the frantic *rrringgg* of an alarm clock at the farmhouse barely visible on the horizon. From the corner of his eye he saw a grass snake slither into a nearby bush, the glitter of eyes as a squirrel skittered up a tree. Despite the fading darkness, the stars seemed brighter and the moon a more vibrant silver.

The sharp scent of hay tickled his nostrils, along with the spicy aroma of apples and pumpkins from one of the nearby farms. He smelled the dusty scent of the gravel road before him and the clean tingle of fresh water being pumped from a well a few miles away.

But more than anything he smelled *her*.

The sweet scent of cotton candy and warm, ripe woman clung to him and filled his head and made him want to haul the bike around and head back to the inn.

To her.

Eight hours, and he still hadn't had enough. When he'd left her, she'd felt as hot and vibrant as the moment he'd met her, and so he'd had a hell of a time tearing himself away. Shit, he'd stayed an extra ten minutes. Touching her with his eyes. Tracing her features. Watching her sleep. Wanting to touch her again with a desperation he'd never felt before.

He gunned the engine faster, eating up gravel at a frenzied pace.

Ten friggin' minutes.

He still couldn't believe it. One had turned to two, and before he'd known it, the alarm on his watch had gone off, sending a jolt of reality through him. He had to get to shelter before he burned to a crisp.

He saw his turn just up ahead. It was little more than a break in the trees, but the path up into the hills was smooth and wide enough for his bike. He slowed and swerved and then he hauled ass again, ducking every so often to avoid a low-hanging branch. Time ticked away and soon pinpoints of light broke through the trees. A few deadly rays needled him here and there as he rushed for cover.

Faster.

Faster.

There.

The trees thinned, and he saw the mouth of the large cave he'd scoped out the night before. A burst of heat washed over him as he broke into a clearing and zoomed the last few feet into the welcoming blackness. The pain blinded him and he skidded to a stop, barely missing the rock wall to his right. The engine ground to a halt and died.

Jake sat there for several seconds, letting the darkness swallow him up and cool his burning flesh. The smell of smoke faded and his vision soon returned. He blinked, and his eyes quickly adjusted to the pitch-black interior.

He shifted into neutral and walked the bike several feet. Rounding a corner, he headed deeper into the cave. The faint sound of running water lured him until the small tunnel he traveled finally opened up into a large black cavern. Water bubbled from an underground spring nearby, dribbling over the rocks and splattering into a small, crystal clear pool.

He killed the engine and parked the bike. Grabbing the leather saddlebags draped over the gas tank, he retrieved his sleeping bag and stretched it out on the dirt floor. He tossed his hat to the ground and pulled off his T-shirt before turning his attention to the rest of his body. He'd suffered only minor burns—his hands, his neck, the bottom of his face—thanks to his unplanned delay back at the inn, but the pain was still excruciating.

Enough to make him wince as he lowered himself onto the soft down.

Enough to distract him from the delicious scent of her that had rubbed off on his skin and the sugary taste that lingered on his lips and the vision—her lusty body flushed and ripe, her eyes closed, her full lips parted on a moan that filled his head.

He was injured. Even more, he was fully charged and satisfied, and so the need for her—for any woman—had been completely and totally satisfied.

But as he stretched out on his back, tucked the edge of his saddlebag beneath his head and closed his eyes, he couldn't seem to relax. The minutes ticked by and instead of focusing on tomorrow—he planned to scope out Town Square and see if he could get a sense for the exact spot where the turning would take place—he found himself thinking about the past few hours.

He heard her soft voice in his head, saw her stretched out beneath him and felt the velvety softness of her skin against his lips. He tasted the ripe essence of her sex as she came against his mouth, and for the first time in his entire existence Jake McCann had the incredible urge to go back for seconds.

Not that he would, of course.

One night was all that he could and would give to any woman.

Even one as sweet and lush as Nikki Braxton.

Particularly one as sweet and lush as Nikki.

The way she'd stared up at him, as if he were a man rather than a monster—as if he were *the* man—made him forget his past and the torment that ate at his soul.

But he wasn't a man.

It was a truth he'd managed to escape for a few blissful moments, but it was back. In the pitch-black blanket of darkness that engulfed him. And the burned flesh that made his head throb. And the bloodlust that gnawed away inside of him. While he'd satisfied his carnal appetite, he'd denied the need to drink.

Barely.

Jake forced aside the unsettling thought and focused on the exhaustion tugging at his body. He needed to sleep. Now more than ever. It was Saturday morning. He had exactly eight days—the following Sunday—until his sire returned to Skull Creek.

As he'd done every morning since he'd started his journey to hunt down the vampire who'd cursed him, he replayed the various outcomes of their final meeting. Death. Destruction. Freedom.

While Jake had never seen the curse broken with his own two eyes, he knew it could be done. He'd met a man just ten years ago who'd claimed he'd once been a vampire. He'd killed his own sire and, in doing so, had freed himself and all the others who'd been turned by that one vampire. It was like a computer virus. Destroy the mainframe and kill the virus at its source.

Jake had never put much faith in people, until he'd become a vampire. He could look into someone's eyes and tell if they were lying.

The man had been telling the truth.

His outrageous story had been the fuel to jump-start Jake. He'd stopped feeling so doomed and started to think that maybe, just maybe, he could set things right.

Garret, Jake's business partner in his motorcycle design business, hadn't been half as hopeful. Garret had been a vampire even longer than Jake and he was much more jaded. He hadn't believed a word of the story—but then, he hadn't been the one to stare into the old man's eyes and see the truth.

Despite Garret's discouragement, Jake had started searching right away. He'd known little about his sire except a name. The name carved into the ornate Spanish dagger that had been used to slice open a vein and force the curse upon Jake.

Sam Black.

Jake had traced every Sam Black recorded in history, marking off names along the way until he'd reached his last prospect.

This was it. *The* Sam Black.

The skilled soldier who'd fought hand-to-hand in several battles for Texas independence. Sam had been notorious for taking souvenirs from his enemies—namely the ornate Spanish daggers supplied by Santa Anna himself.

A bronze plaque sat in Town Square honoring the man who'd been killed by a band of renegade Mexican soldiers just as he'd arrived home from the battle of San Jacinto. The words *To defend is the greatest honor* had been carved into the plaque beneath the outline of a knife.

A Spanish dagger.

Jake fought the anger that whirled inside of him. His hands trembled and he willed his body to relax. He had to calm down. Even more, he had to sleep. To heal.

He breathed, in and out, a steady motion that soon hypnotized. The blackness overwhelmed him.

No tossing. No turning. No dreaming.

He'd regretted the last many times since he'd turned into a vampire. But now, for the first time, he found himself thankful the sleep was so all-consuming.

Jake had a hard enough time pushing Nikki Braxton out of his thoughts when he was conscious and fully aware of every reason why he couldn't—wouldn't—touch her again.

Unconscious? He knew he didn't stand a chance in hell.

THE CLICK OF A LOCK pushed past the fog of sleep that gripped Nikki. The knob creaked and hinges groaned and she smiled. She rolled onto her back, her hand going to the empty sheets next to her. She patted the mattress.

"It's about time you came back to bed."

"If Jimmy John Charles couldn't talk me into the sack—and he had flowers and candy and my favorite denture cream—you can damn well bet I ain't slippin' off the support hose for the likes of you."

The female voice crackled in Nikki's ears and wiped the smile off her face.

It couldn't be.

"Well don't just lay there. I already said no, and that fella you had in here's long gone for now. Get your butt up so's I can change the sheets."

Nikki forced one eye open.

Winona Adkins peered down at her over a thick pair of bifocals.

Winona was the great-grandmother of Eldin Adkins, owner of the Skull Creek Inn and the Elk Lodge's current bingo champion. Eldin's parents had retired to Port Aransas and left him in charge of the inn and Winona.

Winona, who was as headstrong as she was nosy, saw things a little differently. She kept her chubby hands in everything, from the front desk to the housekeeping. She also kept the entire senior ladies' bingo squad informed of the latest gossip. Winona was the squad's president and best friend to Nikki's great-aunt Izzie.

Nikki blinked, hoping the old woman would disappear. Instead the sleepy fog lifted. Her vision cleared, and Winona's features went from blurry and dreamlike to sharp and focused in a matter of seconds.

With a short, chubby body, a head full of snow-white hair and an aren't-you-just-the-sweetest-lookin'-child smile, Winona looked like the classic grandmother. Her hair had been rolled into tight little sausages that covered her head like a football helmet. She wore the familiar flower-print smock, knee-high panty hose and white orthopedic shoes. Aqua Net mingled with Lysol hovered around her. She held a thick ring of keys in one hand and Nikki's panties in the other.

"I—I can explain." So much for a discreet one-night stand. She'd been caught. Not in the act but close enough. And by Winona, of all people.

Her gaze zeroed in on the white cotton undies. Her panties, for cripe's sake.

Her heart pounded as a dozen possible excuses rushed through her head.

I sleepwalked in here and took off my undies.

A saucer full of little green men held me at gunpoint and demanded I take off my undies.

Those aren't really my undies, they're just an illusion.

Her stomach knotted and her throat went tight. *Think,* her brain screamed. She needed a semiplausible story that would salvage as much face as possible.

"I—I was just visiting the man in this room," she blurted. "He's an old friend and we haven't seen each other in such a long time and we had so much to talk about. One minute we were reminiscing, and the next I was out like a light. I've put in so many long days at the salon. I guess they finally caught up with me." She summoned a loud yawn.

"You really *know* the handsome young man who rented this room?"

"Not in the biblical sense," she rushed on, crossing her fingers under the sheet. "We're just friends. Buddies. Old, old acquaintances. I can't believe I just conked right out on him. He slept on the floor and left the bed to me." There. She'd done it. Semiplausible. Now all Winona had to do was bite.

"Of course he did." She nodded. "The minute I opened the door I figured it was something like that."

As lame as it had been, the old woman had bought it. Despite the undies in her hand and the rest of Nikki's clothing that lay in full view of God and everyone.

Nikki waited for a rush of relief, but it didn't come. Instead time pulled at her and suddenly she was back in high school. The only girl who didn't get mentioned on the boy's bathroom wall. The opposite of her mother, who'd gotten her name and number scribbled with frightening regularity.

Nikki had been proud of both at the time. But at the moment...

"I mean, really," Winona went on. "You and that handsome young man? Talk about crazy."

"I don't know if I would go *that* far."

"Are you kidding? I saw him when he checked in last night and, believe me, the two of you are totally wrong for each other." Winona patted her shoulder. "Not that you're chopped liver or anything like that. But you're not anywhere close to centerfold material, and that boy's straight off the pages of one of them *GQ* magazines."

"But opposites attract," Nicki heard herself say.

"Opposites, sugar, as in same species. That boy's from the so-good-looking-it's-a-downright-shame planet. You…well, you're *nice*."

"Men like nice."

Winona gave her a get-out-of-here look. "Men, child, like *nice* if they're looking for a housekeeper or a nanny or a personal assistant. If they're looking to forni-cate…well, nice just doesn't cut it. See, there are two types of women in this world. You've got your drop-dead man teasers like Mae West and Marilyn Monroe. That's the sort a man goes for if he wants a love interest. The pleasers— those poor, desperate souls so starved for love that they'll do just about anything for a man except sleep with him— are the *nice* girls. The sort that'll make you cookies for Valentine's Day instead of doing a striptease and giving a lap dance. The pleasers operate with the misguided notion that the way to a man's heart doesn't involve a direct route through his pants. Not true, on account of a man's heart is located directly in his pants."

She was *not* hearing this.

Not now.

And certainly not from *Winona*.

The woman stood next to Nicki's great-aunt Izzie in the church choir every Sunday morning. And she played Mrs. Claus during the tree-lighting festival at Christmas. And she spearheaded the Pies for Pennies charity bake sale every other Friday.

Like Nikki's aunt Izzie, the old woman was wholesome and sweet and...*nice.*

At the same time, Nikki remembered her mother talking about Winona when she'd been much younger and not so nice. She'd had bright red hair and matching lipstick and, rumor had it, had spent her evenings down at the local saloon.

"Now it's not that men don't like the pleasers," Winona went on. "They do. They just don't see themselves spending eternity with a woman who'd rather cook for them than warm the sheets. Men see those kind of women more like sisters. Somebody to listen when a man feels like whining, to cook when he feels like eating and to boost his ego when he feels down and out. Sure, men get involved with pleasers every lovin' day, but the first whiff they catch of a teaser, bam—" she slapped her hands together "—the pleaser is stuck home on a Friday night watching reruns of *Dog the Bounty Hunter.*" She eyed the T-shirt draped over the back of a nearby chair and shook her head. "Did Bill get you that?"

"I am *not* a pleaser."

Winona smiled. "You should be proud, dear. You're a good girl. Not a thing like your mama." Winona frowned. "Now there's a teaser for you. Jolene's right up there with Pamela Anderson. Poor Izzie. She's always had her hands full with that one. But you...you're a good girl. Why, you're the spittin' image of Izzie herself at your age. That woman was, is and always will be a saint."

"We had sex," Nikki blurted.

"Always putting others first and going out of her way and—excuse me?"

Yeah. *Excuse me?* common sense demanded.

But Nikki's pride had shifted into overdrive, not to mention the sudden urge to defend her mother, and the words starting pouring out before she could stop them. "Me and the good-looking man who checked into this room—Jake," she heard herself say. "His name is Jake and we had sex. Lots of sex." She snatched the white undies from Winona's hand. "He couldn't keep his hands off me."

"The man who checked into *this* room?"

"Jake McCann." Nikki hiked the sheet up under her arms and scooted toward the edge of the bed. "He's totally enamored of me." She pushed to her feet, careful to wrap the sheet around her. "All he thinks about is me." She wiggled to the far corner of the room and retrieved her jeans and T-shirt. "And sex." Winona looked shocked and Nikki gave herself a mental high-five. "It's been really nice talking to you." And then she turned, waddled toward the bathroom and slammed the door shut behind her.

She leaned back against the cool wood and closed her eyes. Her heart beat a frantic rhythm as the past few seconds replayed in her mind.

A smile tugged at her lips.

But the satisfaction she'd felt at blabbing out the truth—the sex part anyhow—quickly fled as she realized that she'd blown her reputation in less than a full minute.

Her mother was going to be the happiest woman in the world.

As for Aunt Izzie…

Nikki didn't want to think about that right now. She couldn't. She was too busy trying to digest Winona's words. A *pleaser?* Is that what the people in town really thought of her? That she was desperate? Starved for love?

If the T-shirt fits…

She'd been starved for sex, not love.

She had plenty of love in her life. She had friends who appreciated her. A mother who adored her. A great-aunt who treasured her.

Granted, the emotions didn't come from a man. But she didn't need a man in her life at this very second. Which was the reason she wasn't at all bummed that Jake McCann had up and left without so much as a few words scribbled on a Post-it.

Sure, she would eventually start dating again and, hopefully, find the right man. But until then she was content being single. She liked her freedom.

She relished it.

Yeah, that explains why you feel disappointed.

Disappointed?

Hardly. She'd gone into last night knowing full well that it was a one-night stand only. A way to burn off the frustration that had been making her completely and totally crazy.

Mission accomplished.

Nikki listened to the footsteps on the other side of the door, followed by the jingle of keys and the heavy creak of hinges. Then everything went silent.

She splashed cold water onto her face and patted it dry. Dropping the sheet, she scrambled into her clothes. A few seconds later, she pulled open the bathroom door.

She spared a quick glance around the room. There was no suitcase. No personal items scattered across the dresser. No clothes hanging in the closet. And definitely no note.

And the problem is?

There was no problem. It had been one night and it was now morning. Which meant over. Done. *Fini.*

She swallowed against the regret creeping up her throat, snatched up her purse and headed for the door.

It was time to forget all about last night and get back to work.

The minute the thought struck, anxiety rushed through her. She glanced at her watch. She was three hours late.

The realization stirred a memory of a small girl sitting up on the couch all night, waiting for her mother to come home. She'd spent so much of her life waiting. And being disappointed.

Not that she resented Jolene. The woman wasn't nearly as irresponsible as she'd once been. As wild as ever, maybe, but at least she no longer made promises she couldn't keep. She loved Nikki, and Nikki loved her, and they'd made peace with the past.

Even so, Nikki liked being on time.

She left the hotel room behind, climbed into her SUV and gunned the engine. She had to get home, get changed and, most of all, get her act together.

That meant forgetting Jake.

A dark, sexy, erotic image rushed at her and brought a

burst of heat to her cheeks. Her nipples tingled. Her thighs ached. Her foot faltered on the gas and she found herself stuck at a red light.

Three hours and counting…

6

It was almost noon by the time Nikki pulled open the swinging glass door and walked into To Dye For.

As was typical on any given Saturday, every seat was filled. From the cutting stations to the shampoo chairs, to the half dozen hair dryers that lined the far wall.

Nikki drew a deep breath and gave an apologetic smile as she bypassed the small reception area and one very unhappy client.

Jean MacGregor was an older woman with lots of wrinkles, dyed brown hair and sparkling silver eye shadow. A coral pantsuit hugged her overweight rump and sizable breasts. A pair of gold cat's-eye glasses hung from a chain around her neck. She smelled of expensive perfume and way too many cigarettes.

"I'm so sorry, Mrs. MacGregor. I lost my keys and then I had a flat tire and then a button fell off my blouse and…" The excuses tumbled out, one after the other, until Jean waved her silent.

"At least you're here now. That man simply can't get my hair to curl the way you do."

That man referred to Charlie Kendall, Nikki's top stylist and best friend, currently teasing up a storm at a nearby station. With great taste, pretty-boy good looks and a footwear wardrobe that would make Carrie from *Sex and the City* jealous, he smacked of gay.

In reality, he was simply the one and only metrosexual in Skull Creek. He had a wife named Darlene, a mortgage and a Chihuahua named Lulu.

"The last time he did me, he used a flatiron and sent me to a city council luncheon with my hair completely straight."

"Sounds trendy."

"I looked like my granddaughter's Mrs. Potato Head." She shook her head. "I'm a big woman, dear. I need big hair to balance out the package."

"Just let me get set up and I'll be right with you." Nikki paused at the reception desk, where a familiar denim-clad butt bobbed behind the Formica counter. "Hey, Dill. What's the problem now?"

The butt morphed into a tall man with sandy blond hair and black-framed glasses. Dillon Cash. Known the world over as Dill thanks to the green pickle suit he'd worn in the kindergarten health pageant. He was now owner and operator of the town's only computer store, located directly across the street from Nikki's salon. While she'd inherited the *nice* label, Dill had *geek* tattooed on his forehead.

"Oh, hey, Nikki." He shoved his thick glasses up onto the bridge of his nose, his pale green eyes barely visible behind the quarter-inch-thick lenses. "I didn't see you."

"I just came in. What's going on?"

"Charlie called this morning. Your hard drive is acting up. I can fix it, but I'll have to take it back to the store with me."

"How long?" The last time she'd had computer problems,

Dill had confiscated her machine for two weeks and she'd been forced to manually schedule several weeks worth of appointments.

"This afternoon."

"Really?" Hope blossomed. Maybe her day wasn't going to hell in a handbasket after all.

He grinned. "Just consider it an early wedding present."

Before the words could register, she heard Charlie's shriek. "Oh, my God. She's here, everyone. She's here!"

"Who?" Nikki turned and glanced behind her as Charlie abandoned his station and rushed toward her, his arms open wide.

He caught her and gave her a delicate smack on the cheek. "To think the ladies' bingo squad actually placed bets that you butter your bread on the wrong side."

Charlie had his long blond hair pulled back into a chic ponytail. He wore a clingy black button-up polyester shirt, à la Tim McGraw, tight faded jeans and a polished pair of what the local cowboys referred to as roach killers. His boots were pointy and shiny with just enough heel to add two inches to his petite five-foot-four frame.

"Why, those old biddies wouldn't know a lesbian if she up and smacked them on their polyester-covered asses." He stepped back, his gaze dropping to the white blouse Nikki had pulled on when she'd stopped off at her house. His smile widened. "Try getting dressed with the lights on next time, honey. Your fiancé will love it."

Nikki glanced down and saw the uneven shirttails and the lone button she'd missed. From the corner of her eye she saw Dillon's ears fire a bright shade of crimson before he turned back to her hard drive and started unhooking wires at the speed of light.

"I was in a hurry," she blurted. Frantically she plucked open the last three buttons and slid them into their designated holes. "I overslept and—" Her words died as her gaze collided with Charlie's and reality hit. "Fiancé? Did you just say fiancé?"

Charlie nodded. "Mr. Tall, Dark and Do Me from the motel. I'd be majorly offended that you didn't kiss and tell since I *am* your closest friend, but I'm too relieved. Not that I thought you were a lesbian. It's just…let's face it, sugar, you've had rotten luck with men." He shrugged and turned.

Nikki headed for her station while Charlie picked up his comb and started teasing the brown hair in front of him. "Which leads me to believe," he went on, "that you attract these losers on a more subconscious level because a) you just don't want to be successful at love or b) you're definitely climbing into bed from the opposite side."

"Couldn't it be a and b?" The question came from the twenty-something brunette buffing nails in the far corner. Familiar green eyes peered over the top of a pair of conservative wire frames.

Cheryl Anne was sweet, bubbly and extremely spoiled. She was also Dillon's kid sister, and therefore, a bit on the geeky side, thanks to DNA. In an effort to shed the big G image, she'd chosen cosmetology rather than pre-law. A choice that hadn't upset her parents in the least because it meant that she could continue to live at home; they'd been heartbroken when Dill had up and moved to his own place at the tender age of twenty-seven. Their father—a local justice of the peace—routinely brought Cheryl Anne lunch and gassed up the sixty-thousand-dollar BMW he'd given her when she'd received her nail license. Their mother stopped by daily to offer the use of her credit cards or bring a round of lattes.

"Maybe she's subconsciously hooking up with losers because she really wants to hook up with a woman," Cheryl Anne went on.

Charlie wagged a comb at her. "That's what I said."

"No, you didn't." Buff, buff. "You said *a* or *b*. Not *a* or *b*, or *a* and *b*."

"That's right." The brown football helmet sitting in Charlie's chair blew at a teased piece of bang that had fallen into her eyes. "You just said *or*."

"I meant *or* or *and*." Charlie picked up a section of hair and worked the comb through it. "It's a figure of speech. It can go either way." He shot Cheryl Anne a glare. "Stop making a fuss. You're taking away from Nikki's special moment."

"Congratulations," echoed down the row of women perched under the dryers.

"We're so happy for you." Cheryl Anne paused midbuff and beamed at Nikki. "I have this totally hot nail kit especially for brides. You have to let me try it out. It has rhinestone appliqués."

"I'm definitely doing your hair," Charlie chimed in. "I'm thinking an updo with pearls—"

"Wait," Nikki cut in, her mind racing. Married? She wasn't getting *married*. Of all the ridiculous notions—

"You're right," Charlie cut into the denial that raced

through her head. "Pearls are so precocious. You're definitely more a rhinestone girl."

"I love rhinestones," Cheryl Anne piped in.

"Me, too," the brown football helmet added.

"I'm not getting married," Nikki blurted. "That's crazy."

"Of course it is. You just got engaged. You probably haven't even set a date. You haven't, have you?" Before Nikki could tell him that she wasn't getting married now—or ever, with the way her luck was running—he rushed on. "While I can understand that he might have just asked you and you haven't really had time to tell everyone, I know with absolute, positive certainty that you wouldn't set a date without telling your best friend. It was bad enough hearing about the engagement from Janice Simcox, who heard it from Rochelle Pryor, who heard it from her brother Mitchell Davis, who heard it from Eldin—"

"Winona," Nikki cut in as the last few frantic minutes started to fall into place—from Dillon's "wedding present" comment to the whole botched lesbian theory. In a small town sex equaled a boyfriend, which equaled till death do us part.

If the woman in question was a *nice* girl, that is.

Charlie planted his hands on his slim hips. "You didn't tell that nosy bigmouth before me, did you?"

"I didn't. I mean, I did. Sort of." Nikki shook her head. "She asked about last night and I told her I was with Jake. But he's just a…a friend," she said. "Not my fiancé."

"Boyfriend. Fiancé. What's the difference?"

"An engagement ring." A woman peeked from beneath one of the dryers. "A great, big, fat rock the size of Texas."

"Amen," the lady sitting next to her added.

"Ring, schming." Charlie waved his comb. "Darlene and I tied the knot without a ring and we've been married almost ten years. She wanted a platinum emerald-cut diamond that I couldn't afford at the time on account of I was just a shampoo boy over at Earline's Hair Salon. So we said 'I do' first, I switched jobs and saved for a ring and now everybody's happy. It's all about economics."

"A girl's gotta have a ring," a woman chimed in. "I say pick out something cheap in the meantime, then replace it later. Wally Picker just got in this new shipment of cubic zirconia." She flashed a newly manicured hand.

Nikki's impending nuptials were quickly forgotten as everyone flocked toward the glittering rock that sat on the woman's finger.

Nikki took the opportunity to flee into the back room. A few seconds later, she set her purse in her locker, pulled on her apron and tried to understand what had just happened.

The entire town thought she was getting married thanks to Winona.

Correction—thanks to Nikki herself.

Sure, she'd never said the word *marriage,* but she'd foolishly admitted to a hot night of sex.

In a small town like Skull Creek, a hot night of sex meant only one thing for a nice girl like Nikki—she was marrying the other half of the dynamic sex duo.

She closed her eyes and smacked her head against the locker. Once. Twice. Her forehead throbbed, but it didn't make her feel any better. No pity party could change things. There was only one way to get herself out of this mess.

She had to tell the truth. Everything. All the sordid details. From severe sexual deprivation to hormone-driven acquiescence to mouthing off out of sheer humiliation.

Then again, she'd tried this morning—sort of—and it had gotten her this close to an updo and rhinestone bridal nails.

Besides, if she spilled her guts, everyone would realize that she'd gotten busy with a total stranger. Sure, she was a grown woman. An independent, red-blooded, normal woman fully capable of having a safe one-night stand. An explanation that would fly if she were in any major city in the free world. But this was a small Texas town where gossip was as abundant as cow manure.

Nikki had spent her entire life trying to crawl out of Jolene's shadow.

One night would push her right back in if people were to learn the truth.

Better to go with the flow, play at a relationship—a long distance relationship since Jake had already left town—and then slowly fade him out of the picture.

With her mind made up, she left the safety of the back room and headed for her workstation. A few minutes later, Mrs. MacGregor, swathed in a black cape, parked in Nikki's stylist chair.

"So you'll be bringing him to the fairgrounds tonight for the cook-off?" Charlie spared Nikki a glance.

"I—"

"Of course she will be," Cheryl Anne piped in. "Everybody will be there. Talk about the perfect time to prove to the world that you're not grieving over Bill."

"You have to come," Charlie reiterated. "Darlene and I

will be there, and I would love for her to meet this guy. Not that she supported the lesbian theory, mind you. Not one hundred percent—omigod, are you blushing?"

Blushing? Nikki glanced in the mirror and noted the flush that crept up her neck and spread into her cheeks.

"You are," Charlie rushed on before she could blurt out a semiplausible excuse. As if she could even think of one. As if she could think, period. The past night kept rushing through her mind. Jake and the sex. The sex and Jake. Her nerves buzzed. Her hands trembled.

Forget.

"Too cute," Charlie added. "Listen, I could do your hair for tonight. Something special to impress the new Mr. Braxton. I'm thinking long and tousled."

"What about pulled up?" Cheryl Anne rolled a bottle of Come and Get Me red nail polish between her palms. "Men like a bare neck."

"Men like the I-just-rolled-out-of-bed look more," Charlie told her.

"What makes you the expert when it comes to men?" Cheryl Anne arched one waxed eyebrow.

"I happen to have a penis."

"You might have all the equipment, but your heart isn't in it. You eat quiche."

"I also cook it, but that's beside the point." He planted his hands on his hips. "I'm still a man and I say we do long and tousled."

"I vote for pulled up."

"I like braids myself," Mrs. MacGregor offered. "What about you, Nikki? What do you think?"

I think I'd like another night. Just to see if the second would be half as good as the first.

The thought pushed its way in and Nikki pushed it right back out. *Over, remember?* She drew a shaky breath and tried to concentrate on the here and now. *Just go along and fade out slowly.*

"So?" Charlie prodded. "Long and tousled? Updo? Braids?"

She grabbed a mixing bowl. "Braids are nice."

And useful, she added silently.

If her plan backfired, she could always make a noose with one, slip it over her head and end her misery once and for all.

7

IT WAS EIGHT O'CLOCK by the time Nikki said goodbye to her last customer and switched off the neon Open sign in the front window.

Late for a typical Saturday; the salon closed at five.

But not late enough for this particular night.

She'd taken things slow throughout the day—painstakingly so. Since her computer was now sitting in Dillon's brightly lit shop across the street—he was notorious for putting in the late hours thanks to a nonexistent social life—she'd spent an extra hour manually scheduling appointments. She'd cut and styled client after client at the pace of a turtle. She'd even done extra lowlights—free of charge—on her last customer. And a deep-conditioning treatment. And a few hair extensions. She'd also taken a lengthy break to head over to the hardware store to pick up some swatches for new paint colors for her kitchen. While she'd managed to close three hours later than usual, she was still finished early enough to make an appearance at the cook-off.

She glanced at the balloon bouquet—a cluster of pink and white latex surrounding a silver Mylar *Congratulations*—sitting at her station. A plate of homemade chocolate chip cookies sat next to it, along with a basket of fresh-baked blueberry muffins, a platter of Ms. Langtree's prize-winning fudge and a monstrous foil-wrapped meat loaf.

All engagement presents from her loyal customers.

She'd actually felt a small sliver of excitement when the balloons had first arrived.

Followed by a mental ass-kicking that had started with a very loud *Earth to Nikki! You don't have a fiancé. You don't have a boyfriend. You don't even have a cat.*

Which meant she was going to the cook-off solo—and every other event during the weeklong Founder's Day celebration, including Friday night's Fall Ball.

The couples event of the year.

No one missed the dance. Even Golden Acres, the local seniors home, bussed its residents—a lively bunch of men and women known as the Greyhounds—over for the event.

Nikki had assumed she would go with Bill before she'd discovered the twin skeletons of infidelity hanging in his closet.

Not that she was disappointed. She was more relieved. At least she'd found out before she'd gotten even closer to him. Besides, the breakup had been just the jump-start she'd needed to get on with her life. And her future.

Without a man.

She glanced at the clock again before busying herself around the shop. She straightened hair products and Windexed the front windows. She waved back at Dillon, who waved at her from across the street. She stared at the new paint swatches and tried to envision each of them covering the walls in her kitchen. She knew her mother would go for the red—namely because Jolene had said so more than once since learning about the house—while Aunt Izzie would choose her usual yellow. And Nikki? She liked both colors and at least a half dozen others.

But more than worrying over the right shade, Nikki found herself trying to come up with an excuse to get her out of the current predicament.

She would tell Charlie and Cheryl Anne that Jake had had to cut his visit short because of a work-related emergency and he'd already left town to go back home.

Not that she knew where "home" was.

While they'd had incredible sex, he was still little more than a stranger.

The truth should have sent a rush of embarrassment through her, but her brain excluded the stranger part and snagged on the sex. A vivid image rushed at her, and she saw him looming above her, his face dark and intense, his eyes gleaming in the moonlight. She felt the press of his weight as he spread her thighs even wider and pushed deep.

Nikki bit her lip against the sudden ache between her legs. Crazy, right? She'd done the deed. Satisfied the need. The only thing she should feel at the moment was complete and total satisfaction.

She didn't.

Before she could dwell on the thought, her cell phone rang and the paint swatches scattered.

"I'm pulling in the back parking lot," Jolene's deep, sultry voice came over the line. "Meet me at the back door." Click.

Jolene? Here? *Now?*

Nikki scrambled for her purse and retrieved a tube of lipstick. She swiped her lips and rubbed them together. Pulling out her ponytail holder, she flipped her head upside down and rifled her hands through her hair. She'd just righted herself to spray her newly fluffed hair when she heard the knock on the back door. She stabbed the button on the freeze spray and whirled it around her head. Chucking the can, she rushed toward the rear of the building.

On the way, she undid an extra button on her blouse. Taking a deep breath and pasting on her most alluring smile, she flipped the dead bolt and hauled open the back door.

"It's about time. I'm melting out here." Jolene Braxton looked every bit her forty-six years and then some thanks to one too many late nights.

But while she was worn around the edges, she was still a beautiful woman. She had thick blond hair and creamy white skin and a trim figure. She wore a snug red dress and matching high heels. Bright red fingernails glittered in the dim light as she fanned her face.

"What in tarnation took you so long?"

Nikki beamed. "Just freshening up."

Heavily rimmed eyes raked her from head to toe. "You really should try wearing a little more makeup, dear. You look washed out. And that hair…try some mousse or something. It's much too flat." Jolene walked past her.

"I've been working all day, Mom." She turned to follow the woman toward the front of the shop. "What's up?" As if she didn't know.

"I had to stop by and see for myself." Her gaze riveted on the cluster of engagement gifts. "Holy hell, it *is* true."

Her chest pumped as if she were trying to take a (deep) breath but just couldn't seem to drag enough air into her lungs. "You're engaged," she said accusingly.

"I am not."

"Yes, you are." Her gaze collided with Nikki's. "Izzie's been in the kitchen all afternoon."

"Oh, no."

"Oh, yes. She made a pie. An *apple* pie," Jolene delivered the final verdict.

Uh-oh. Apple pie was Izzie's specialty and it meant only one thing.

The bridal march played in Nikki's head and she closed her eyes. "She talked to Winona, didn't she?"

"Of course she did. That old woman couldn't wait to call and spread the news. Izzie practically fell all over herself rushing to the oven. Meanwhile, I had a coronary."

Nikki waited for the standard "This is too quick" speech that most mothers would have delivered upon hearing of their daughter's sudden engagement. "You don't know this man. Give it some time. Then if you still feel the same way…"

But Jolene wasn't most mothers.

"Marriage sucks," she told Nikki. Not that Jolene knew firsthand. She'd never actually been married. Her longest relationship had lasted all of five weeks. Then she'd gotten pregnant and he'd taken off. The end. "Why you would want to go and do something so foolish, I'll never know—"

"I'm not getting married," she cut in. "Really. I'm not."

"But Izzie said Winona said that you were caught cavorting at the motel with—"

"It wasn't like that. He's not my fiancé." Nikki thought

about telling Jolene the truth but then nixed the idea. While she didn't want to be the nice girl Winona had made her out to be, she wasn't ready to paint a scarlet letter on her chest and accompany Jolene down to the nearest honky-tonk. "He's just a…a friend."

A smile tilted the corners of Jolene's mouth. "I knew that old woman must have gotten it wrong. No way would my baby do something so stupid. Men are great, cupcake. Loads of fun. But never, *ever* sign your life over to one of them. You might as well hang a sign on your back that says Property Of." Jolene kissed Nikki's cheek and then rubbed at the lipstick. "You're pale, cupcake. You really should try wearing a little more blush. Maybe a bronzer." She turned and eyed her reflection in one of the mirrors before reaching into her bag for a tube of Crimson Delight. "You're a pretty girl. You should show off a little more." Her gaze dropped to Nikki's standard black skirt and white blouse. "Get a little fancy. Wear something dramatic. Something red."

Nikki liked red as much as the next person, but it wasn't her signature color. "I'll do that."

"Get rid of all this drab and go for bold," Jolene went on, shoving the tube back into her clutch. "And spicy." Her gaze caught the paint swatches that lay scattered on the countertop. "Something like this." She fingered one of them. "Does this come in a lipstick?"

"It comes in latex. I'm trying to decide on new colors for my kitchen."

"Oh." Jolene wrinkled her nose. "Why you're so dead set on renovating that big mess, I'll never know. Why couldn't you have bought yourself a nice condo or something? They still have that one available just a few doors down from me."

Which is why Nikki hadn't opted for the condo. That and the fact that when she gazed out the front window of her dream home, she wanted to see lots of trees rather than a bunch of divorced forty-somethings skinny-dipping in the community hot tub.

"The house is really great—or it will be by the time I'm finished with it. Renovating is sort of fun."

Jolene wrinkled her nose again. "Make sure you wear gloves when you're painting. The fumes will kill your skin." She glanced at her watch. "Jesus, would you look at the time? I have to go. I've got a dinner date. New guy. I just had to stop and make sure you hadn't gone off the deep end. Hugs and kisses." She whirled, and in a blur of red she was gone.

Nikki had just shut and locked the back door and was headed toward the stockroom when she heard the squeal of tires and the grunt of a familiar exhaust.

Her day just kept getting worse.

Frantic, she swiped the back of her hand over her lips and rubbed at the lipstick. She combed her fingers through her hair and tried to pat it back under control. She'd just rebuttoned the top buttons on her blouse when she heard the faint knock.

The smell of apple pie hit her as she pulled open the door to see her great-aunt.

Izzie was a tiny old woman with a head full of snow-white hair and a smile that warmed Nikki from the inside out. There wasn't a hint of makeup on her face; she believed in a woman's natural, God-given beauty. She wore a pale floral-print dress and white patent leather shoes. She smelled of vanilla extract and cinnamon and gas fumes.

Nikki stared past the old woman to see Winona's ancient Buick idling in the background.

"Thank the Lord." Izzie thrust the warm pie into Nikki's hands. "I was afraid I was going to get here too late. My lattice crust broke and I had to redo it. And then Winona was rushing me on account of we've got bingo tonight, and I got nervous and the crust broke *again*. But all's well that ends well. I'm here." She beamed. "My baby niece is getting *married*."

"About that—" Nikki started, but Izzie cut her off.

"I told you not to jump the gun and buy that big old house all by yourself. You should have waited. That way you and Jake could have picked out your place together. Oh, well. You can always sell it."

She glanced down at the pie and swallowed. "Thanks." Thanks? But she and Jake weren't picking out anything. And she certainly wasn't selling her house. "It's not what you think. I'm not getting married."

"What?" The old woman's brows drew together. "But Winona said that she found you and your panties and—"

"That is," she cut in, "I'm not getting married at this moment. It's just an engagement. A really long engagement."

"Nonsense." Relief gleamed in the old woman's eyes. "There's no reason to wait when you're sure. You are sure, aren't you?"

No. "Yes." She nodded. "He's definitely the one."

"Good, because when Winona told me what a compromising position she found you in, I knew there was no way that you would have been doing God knows what with God knows who if you weren't serious. My Nikki would never do such a thing. Now Jolene…" She shook her head. "I wish I knew where I went wrong with that one."

"You didn't go wrong. You did your best. Mom's just…Mom."

Izzie's expression softened and she smiled. "At least I got you right. So—" she smiled "—have you decided on a date? A place? What about the wedding colors? Mary Margaret's daughter had hot-pink, and it was the most garish thing I've ever seen. You should really go for something bright and cheerful. Yellow. I love yellow. You could carry a bouquet of daisies. Or buttercups. Or maybe both."

She looked so hopeful, so happy, that Nikki found herself nodding. "Sounds great. Say, shouldn't you be going?" Nikki peered past Izzie and waved at the old woman sitting behind the wheel of the gigantic silver land barge. "You wouldn't want to be late to bingo."

"I do have to get going. I just couldn't concentrate until I spoke to you myself and dropped by a little token of my happiness." She kissed Nikki again—and doubled the guilt churning inside of her. "I'll see you tomorrow morning, dear, for Sunday breakfast." Her eyes twinkled. "I'm making blueberry waffles."

Uh-oh. The last time Izzie had made waffles, Nikki had been voted Most Studious her senior year of high school. Jolene had protested—she'd been voted Most Talented with a Mascara Wand—by having dry toast. It had been the most uncomfortable meal of Nikki's life.

"I can't wait." Nikki watched as Izzie turned and waddled toward the car before shutting and locking the door. She barely ignored the urge to down a gallon of perm solution—anything to end the misery right here and now.

She settled for drowning her troubles in Izzie's prize-winning pie. The first bite sent a rush of sugar to her brain that killed the guilt and stirred a burst of happy. Mmm… Things weren't really that bad. Nothing she couldn't deal with.

By the time she'd taken her tenth bite, her brain buzzed and she didn't feel half as guilty. Rather, she felt desperate. She'd saddled herself with a fictitious boyfriend and she needed a plausible story to explain him. And fast.

Name? Jake McCann.

Occupation? Independent consultant—of what she wasn't sure, but with any luck, folks would be too impressed by his title to ask.

Native Houstonian.

They'd met online and their personalities had magically clicked.

They both liked picnics.

They both loved *Survivor*.

They both enjoyed football and rooted for the Houston Texans.

They'd been friends first, and when Bill had hightailed it to Vegas, Jake had rushed to comfort her. The friendship had evolved and—bam!—they were now hopelessly devoted to one another.

They weren't sure how they were going to work out the long-distance aspect—he did live over three hours away—but both were willing to try.

If only.

The thought followed her as she stored what was left of the pie, as well as the other goodies, in the small portable refrigerator. She retrieved her purse and walked toward the back door. Crazy, she knew. The last thing she should feel was regret for a man she didn't even know. Sure, they'd had sex. Spectacular sex. But it was still just a one-night stand. Meaning it was now over and she should get on with her life.

Forget.

If only.

The notion struck again, followed by a very vivid image from last night.

She saw Jake looming over her, felt his rough hands trailing down her stomach, between her legs. He parted her slick folds and one finger slid deep and…

Nikki forced aside the memory and flicked off the lights. Her hands trembled on the knob as she punched the lock and pulled the door shut behind her.

The sun had set hours ago, and the parking lot sat dark and ominous beyond the reach of the back porch light. Nikki made her way toward her SUV and hit the unlock button.

She climbed behind the wheel and tried to ignore the strange sensation that danced along her nerve endings. She'd felt it last night when she'd been at the cotton candy booth. An awareness.

Someone was watching her.

He was watching her.

If—

She squelched the traitorous thought before it could take root this time.

Jake McCann had already left town.

Passing through, he'd said.

Thankfully.

Otherwise, he would have been front and center, telling everyone he wasn't her boyfriend, much less her fiancé. Or even her friend.

The entire town would then think that she was nothing more than a chip off the old chopping block. A carbon copy of her mother.

She wasn't.

Her mother had liked the endless string of men. The variety. The excitement. She'd been a small-town girl with big-city ideas and she'd been bored as hell.

Nikki, however, liked living in a small town. She liked eating the same blueberry muffin for breakfast every morning and seeing the same faces day after day. Just like her aunt Izzie.

Sort of.

She didn't like the routine quite as much as her aunt, but she wasn't itching to spread her wings, either. She was somewhere in the middle.

Stuck.

Not for long. She couldn't keep putting up a front for both women. Eventually she would have to decide. Izzie or Jolene? Good or bad?

She'd felt bad to the bone last night.

Thanks to Jake.

She hung a right and started down Main Street, her thoughts going to him. He was probably in the next city by now. Or even a different state. Who knew? He could have crossed the state line into Arkansas. Or Louisiana. Maybe he was playing the roulette table in Lake Charles at this very second. Or eating at some five-star restaurant in Little Rock.

Or sucking down beers at the Shade Tree.

Nikki slammed on the brakes, her gaze riveted on the black-and-chrome motorcycle parked in front of the local sports bar located just a block from her salon.

Her heart jumped into her throat and her pulse raced and her hands tightened on the steering wheel.

He couldn't be...

He wasn't...

Even as denial echoed through her head, dread settled in the pit of her stomach.

There was no denying the motorcycle. Even more, there was no denying the sudden zing of electricity that snaked up her spine.

Jake McCann *was* still here. And Nikki was totally screwed.

JAKE KNEW IT WAS HER long before he felt the tap on his shoulder and heard her soft, "Hey."

Ever since he'd ridden back into town just after sunset, he'd felt her—a sizzle of vibration that swept his nerve endings and pulsed in the back of his brain. The feeling had sucker punched him last night at the carnival when he'd spotted her, and the sex had only intensified things.

Shit.

If anything, she should have fallen off his radar by now. She should be home in bed. Exhausted. Recuperating after he'd drained her of so much energy.

Instead she stood directly behind him, her luscious scent filling his nostrils. Her soft breaths echoed in his ears. Sexual hunger bubbled inside of her, and his gut tightened with renewed need.

Yep, he needed her, all right.

Not *her,* mind you.

Sure, her hair was some of the softest he'd ever felt and he'd liked the soft gasp she'd made when he'd stroked the spot just below her navel. And, hell yes, he'd liked the way she'd stared up at him, into him, when he'd been inside of her, as if she could see past the chains that bound him to the man beneath.

He forced aside the damnable thought. Sex, he reminded himself. There wasn't anything special about Nikki other than the fact that she was female.

That's what he told himself as he turned and his gaze collided with hers.

For a split second, he wanted to dive headfirst into the warm, golden pools that reminded him of the bottle of Jack Daniels sitting behind the bar.

Potent.

Intoxicating.

Trouble.

When he'd first discovered the truth of what Sam Black had done to him, he'd been terrified and disgusted and mad as hell. He hadn't wanted to believe he'd become a monster and so he'd crawled into a bottle to escape. The booze had helped him forget and pretend that he was still human.

For a little while.

But then the hunger had caught up to him, and since he'd been drunk off his ass and weak, it had overwhelmed him to the point that he'd done the unspeakable.

Almost.

But then Garret had shown up. The vampire had hauled Jake to his feet and fed him until his sanity had returned. And then Garret had taught him how to never, ever let the hunger get the best of him.

He steered clear of the hard stuff now, afraid to let down his defenses. Terrified to lose his hard-won control.

The way he had last night.

No. Not completely.

Not ever, *ever* again.

"What are you doing here?" she asked before he could think too hard about his past.

"Talking to you, darlin'."

"I don't mean here—" she stared around "—I mean *here.* I thought you were just passing through."

"I am. I'm here through next Sunday and then I'll be leaving."

"*Next* Sunday?" At his nod, her gaze lit with panic. "But that's eight days from now."

"A woman who can count." He winked. "I like that."

"*Eight,*" she repeated as if she were still trying to absorb the fact. "But you can't... I can't... I—I thought you were leaving," she finally blurted. "That's the only reason I slept with you." When he arched an eyebrow at her, she added,

"Okay, so it wasn't the only reason, but it was the deciding factor. One night. That was it."

"That was it."

"Exactly. Except now you're here and everyone thinks you're my fiancé. I know," she rushed on, "this is supposed to be one of those no-strings-attached things, and it is. They think you're my fiancé, but that doesn't mean you have any obligation to me. You don't. It's just that Winona—she's the grandmother of the guy who owns the inn—walked in to clean the room and found me naked and then she assumed I couldn't have spent the night having sex because I'm more the buddy type of woman and it hurt my feelings and I couldn't help myself, I told her the truth. But then she assumed that since I am more the buddy type of woman I wouldn't just hook up with anyone so I must have a new boyfriend and then by the time I walked into work—bam—I had a new fiancé."

"You're kidding, right?"

She nodded. "Hazards of a small town. Not that it's any big deal. Or it wasn't any big deal. I was just going to pretend like we were having a long-distance relationship and then fade you out of the picture slowly, but here you are. *Here.*" Her lips trembled and her cheeks flushed and he could practically see the thoughts racing through her mind. "What am I going to do?"

"You could tell the truth."

She seemed to think for a second, and there was no mistaking the fear that flashed in her gaze. "Not an option," she finally said with a firm shake of her head.

"Find someone else."

"Half the town has already seen you."

"So hire an escort who looks like me."

"Small town, remember? The closest thing we have to an escort service is old man Hamilton. He can waltz like nobody's business. All of the senior ladies want to go to the annual silver cotillion with him, and so he goes with the woman who makes the biggest and the tastiest pot roast. I'm out of luck because a) he doesn't have as much hair or as many teeth as you and b) I can't make a pot roast to save my life." She caught and held his stare. "I need you," she told him.

Forget it. It was there on the tip of his tongue, but the word *need* kept echoing in his brain. As crazy as the whole story seemed, it was true.

She really and truly needed him.

"I'll make it worth your while," she added. "I can pay. Just name your price." He could see the desperation in her eyes and hear it in the tremble of her voice.

And damned if he could resist.

"Okay," he told her. "Here it is." And his lips touched hers.

8

HE WANTED SEX.

The truth echoed in Nikki's head as she left Jake sitting at the bar and headed for the ladies' room. She could feel his gaze on her back. Her skin prickled and excitement chased up and down her spine. Her lips still tingled from the feel of his and her heart pounded double time. She pushed through the swinging door marked Gals and headed for the sink. She shoved her hands beneath the faucet, splashed her heated face and tried to come to terms with what had just happened.

Jake had agreed to accompany her on various outings around town and play the loving boyfriend for the next week in exchange for more of last night.

She still couldn't believe he'd made the offer. Hell, she couldn't believe she'd asked him to help her in the first place. But she'd been so freaked out on hearing that he intended to hang around town a full week that she'd had to do something.

She'd asked and he'd kissed and now they were officially a couple.

She reached for a paper towel and dabbed her face.

He wanted *sex.*

Correction—he wanted exciting, phenomenal, stupendous sex. The kind they'd had last night.

But that had tipped the scales toward the fabulous because it had been spontaneous. Wild. Crazy. *Temporary.* She hadn't had to worry about what to make him for breakfast. Or what to say when he left. Or when they would see each other again. Or *if* they would ever see each other.

There'd been none of the typical obsessing over outfits or hairstyles or exciting conversation topics.

Because last night had been last night. There'd been no tomorrow where Jake McCann had been concerned, and so she'd been able to let her hair down and be herself.

As soon as the thought struck, she pushed it right back out. She hadn't been herself last night. She'd been sex-starved. A responsible, sane, normal person who'd been pushed to the limit by stress and deprived hormones.

Today she was back to normal and this…this was just a business arrangement. Not a real relationship. It wasn't as if they were going to send out Christmas cards together or buy monogrammed towels. In seven days Jake would be history and she would be back to her search for a nice, normal, forever kind of relationship, and so the worry over tomorrow wasn't a factor. Rather, this particular situation involved sex only.

Just like last night.

She stared into the mirror and noted her flushed cheeks and trembling lips. Her eyes gleamed with a bright, hungry light. Anticipation bubbled inside and pumped her heart faster and she frowned.

It wasn't as if she was looking forward to hot, wild sex.

with a man she hardly knew. She was simply happy that Jake had agreed to help her preserve her reputation.

Relieved.

If only relief didn't feel a lot like full-blown, pulse-pounding excitement.

"I SWEAR YOU'RE TRYING to give me a heart attack." Nikki eyed the black-and-chrome motorcycle parked at the curb just outside of the Shade Tree.

"It's just a bike, sugar." Jake straddled the leather seat and patted the space behind him. "It won't bite."

"No, but it might splatter me all over Main Street." Nikki shook her head. "Forget it."

"I've got an extra helmet and I'm a safe driver." His compelling silver gaze locked with hers, and her heart started to beat even faster. In a flash, she saw herself climbing behind him, sliding her arms around and holding tight. Her fingers itched to feel the soft cotton of his T-shirt, and her chest hitched.

As if he read the thoughts racing through her mind, he smiled.

She frowned, breaking the temporary spell. "I'll take my SUV and meet you there."

"Sort of defeats the purpose, doesn't it? If we're supposed to be a couple, we shouldn't be using separate means of transportation. If I'm crazy over the moon for you, there's no way I'd let you drive your own vehicle."

And if she were "crazy over the moon" for him, no way would she not climb onto the back of his bike.

"Come on." His deep voice coaxed her. "It'll be fun."

It would, and that was the problem in itself. Nikki Braxton didn't throw caution to the wind in the name of fun. She never had and she never would.

She colored inside the lines. Followed the rules. Cherished her routine.

"My hair will get messed up." It was a lame excuse considering she hadn't so much as brushed her hair all day. But hey, she was a hairdresser. With any luck, he would think that sort of thing was important to her.

"It's already messed up." He eyed her. "And it looks damned sexy."

Then again, he had a point. If they were really and truly a couple, they would be inseparable.

"Give me the helmet."

She took the silver contraption he handed her and popped it on her head. She started to adjust the chin straps and he climbed off.

"I can do it myself," she told him when he reached for her.

"Have you ever adjusted a helmet before?"

"I've adjusted a bicycle helmet."

He grinned, a full-blown ear-to-ear that did funny things to her heartbeat. "This is different, sugar. The straps are wider and the catch is larger." His fingers grazed her chin as he took the straps from her hand and fastened the ends. He adjusted the fit, his knuckle grazing here, his thumb brushing there, and her skin tingled at each point of contact. Her stomach flipped and her breath caught. "There," he finally declared, his hands falling away. "That wasn't so bad, was it?"

Her gaze rooted on his lips and she had the sudden urge

to kiss him. A full, deep, forget-everything-and-everyone kiss. "I…" She licked her lips and ignored the urge. "Can we just get this over with?" She motioned to the bike.

A grin tugged at the corner of his mouth. "Anxious to get to the good part?" A teasing light danced in his eyes, along with something dark and intense that made her want to rip off her clothes and jump him right then and there.

She stiffened. "Don't flatter yourself. It wasn't that good."

"You're right, sugar." He winked. "It wasn't even close to good." *It was great.*

His lips didn't move on the last part. Rather, his voice echoed *inside* her head.

Wait a second. Back the tractor up….

Of course his lips had moved. She'd *heard* him. Loud and crystal clear. And in order for her to hear him, his lips *had* to have moved.

An image flashed in her mind of Jake poised above her, his head thrown back, his eyes closed, his mouth open and his fangs extended….

"Let's go." His deep voice lured her back to reality, away from the crazy detour her thoughts were trying to take. He turned and straddled the bike.

Nikki ignored the strange tingling in her stomach and climbed on behind him. Sliding her arms around, she clutched the soft cotton of his shirt and braced herself as he kick-started the bike. In a matter of seconds they were speeding down Main Street. The wind rushed at her face and pushed away the disturbing thoughts until the only thing on her mind was holding tight to the man in front of her.

Just a man, she told herself.

If only she really and truly believed it.

"I TOLD YOU SHE WASN'T a lesbian." The man's voice, soft and distant, sliced through the usual carnival sounds and slid into Jake's ear.

His gaze skimmed past the ticket booth where he waited with Nikki and pushed through the crowd until he spotted the couple several yards away. Well out of hearing range.

For anyone but Jake, that is.

The sounds faded as he tuned in to the couple who approached. He heard the soft draw of the woman's breath and the steady crunch of gravel beneath the man's high-dollar snakeskin boots.

"That'll be six dollars, please." A voice drew Jake's attention and he turned toward the ticket stand.

Nikki reached for her wallet, but Jake was already laying a twenty down on the counter.

"Handsome *and* a gentleman," the ticket lady said as she took the money and turned to retrieve change. "I'm impressed." She counted out a handful of one-dollar bills for Jake. "Good for you, honey." She handed the money to Jake and winked at Nikki.

"Thanks, Marie."

The woman eyed Jake again and smiled. "My pleasure."

"I could have paid," Nikki told Jake as he pressed his hand into the small of her back and ushered her past the entrance gate.

"You wanted a boyfriend, and in my book, a boyfriend pays."

"But this isn't for real. While you made a commitment to pretend, you didn't agree to cover any expenses. You're already doing me a big favor. I don't want to be a hardship."

"Trust me, I can afford it. Besides, this isn't a favor." He eyed her and her bottom lip trembled ever so slightly. "You'll be paying me back soon enough."

"Still," she started, a stubborn light firing her eyes. "I don't think—"

"I'll run a tab and we can settle up later."

"Okay." She licked her lips. "So when you said 'I can afford it,' did you mean 'I'm filthy rich and this is chump change,' or 'I'll have to skip tomorrow's Starbucks, but it's doable'? Not that it matters," she rushed on. "It's just, I don't really know much about you, and since you did agree to play the dutiful boyfriend, I probably should know a little bit about you, like what you do for a living."

"I design custom motorcycles. I do the actual construction and my partner does the design."

"What's his name?"

"Garret. Garret Sawyer."

"We've got some Sawyers here in Skull Creek. Mabel and Earl. They live over on Maple and Fifth. Really nice people."

"I doubt they're any relation."

"You never know. So where's home base?"

"We don't really have one. We've been working out of a small shop in Houston for the past few months while we do some work for a few clients in the area. Before that we were in Georgia for a while. Before that it was Miami. Nashville. L.A."

"So you really are just passing through."

He grinned. "I don't lie, sugar. Even if it's a one-night stand."

"I didn't mean that. It's just, sometimes people say what other people want to hear—"

"It's called lying." He shook his head. "And I don't."

Then tell me why you really kissed me last night at the carnival. Why me?

The comment was there in her head, glittering in the whiskey-colored depths of her eyes, but it never made it to her full pink lips. Instead a man's voice rang out as the couple who'd been having the lesbian conversation finally reached them.

"If it isn't the best hairdresser this side of the Rio Grande," the man said.

A smile touched Nikki's lips as she turned. "This is Charlie," Nikki told Jake. "We work together."

"Actually, I work. Nikki prances in late." He winked. "And this shameless hussy by my side is my wife Darlene. Say hi, honey."

"Hi, there, honey." Despite her suggestive words, it was obvious the woman was head over heels for her husband. She leaned into his side, and a warmth fired her expression as she poked him in the ribs. "And don't call me a hussy."

"What about shameless?"

"That works." She winked. "Lucky for you."

Jake smiled. "Pleased to meet you both." He shook Charlie's hand and then his wife's.

"So have you been on the Master Blaster? Charlie and I rode it about fifteen minutes ago and I swear my stomach still hasn't calmed down."

"Actually, we just got here." Nikki glanced around. While there were a few people moving here and there, the majority of the crowd seemed to be clustered around a large white tent several yards away. "What's going on?"

"Sherman Calhoun is this close to being pushed off his throne."

"So that's what the crowd is all about," Nikki said, glancing toward the gathering throng of people. "Sherman is the reigning rib king," she told Jake.

"When folks heard he was competing, advance ticket sales tripled," Darlene added. "Everyone in town wants a front-row seat for this."

"Why is that?" Jake asked.

Nikki grinned. "Big cities have professional sports, we've got public humiliation."

"Does he usually cry like that when he doesn't get his way?" Jake asked ten minutes later as they stared at the spectacle on stage. A chubby Sherman stood next to the town's mayor, tears rolling down his cheeks as he clutched his second-place ribbon.

"Usually he throws punches," Nikki said. "Or chairs. Or barbecue forks. One time he even pulled out his shotgun and tried to take out Marvin Helmsley during a rib-eye grilling competition. I've seen him spit and cuss, but the crying's a first."

"It's part of his anger management therapy," Darlene offered. "Remember last Fourth of July when he lost the brisket competition? He got so angry that he shoved a sparkler down the back of Jim Limpkin's pants and set him on fire."

"Oh, yeah. Poor Jim couldn't sit down for months."

"Of course, now he's got the best tush in town, so all the pain was worth it," Darline said. When Jake frowned, she added, "He had a really flat butt before. But after the sparkler incident, his insurance coughed up money for skin grafts and implants. Now he fills out a pair of Wranglers the way a man should. It was definitely the best day of his life, which brings us back to Sherman. Jim was so thankful that instead of pressing charges, he gave Sherman a reward. Sherman wanted to buy a new barbecue pit, but his wife Maureen made him sign up for anger management classes at the local junior college. Anyhow, now instead of blowing his lid, as an effective means of releasing his stress, he cries."

Jake watched as the man shook his head, let out a loud wail and rushed off the stage, a box of Kleenex in his hands.

"Looks like the show's over," Charlie said, clapping his hands together. He slid an arm around Darlene's shoulder. "What say we call it a night and leave these two lovebirds to fend for themselves?"

The two exchanged glances and she nodded. "Yes, I am a little tired."

"It's barely ten," Nikki protested, as if the sudden thought of being alone with Jake made her nervous.

It did. He could feel the emotion rolling off her, along with a rush of excitement.

The knowledge stirred his lust, and it took extreme effort to force a casual smile and say goodbye to Nikki's friends.

His hands itched. And his gut clenched. And his mouth watered. He wanted to kiss her. Bad.

"So what do you say?" She turned toward him. "Are you hungry?"

"You wouldn't believe."

"I was talking about the ribs."

He tamped down on his raging lust and ignored the urge to reach out. Barely.

The realization made him stiffen. Because Jake didn't let his urges—not the thirst for blood or the unquenchable desire for sex—get the best of him. Yes, he nurtured them both, but only as a means of controlling them. To keep them from controlling him.

He called the shots.

But then Nikki looked at him with those wide, sparkling eyes and the only thing he wanted to do was dive straight in and forget everything else.

"They're the best ribs in town," she prodded, a grin tugging her full lips. "You won't be sorry."

But he already was. The last thing—the very *last* thing—he needed was to lose his self-control over a woman. Especially a wholesome, I-want-it-all type like Nikki.

At the same time, it had been a helluva long time since he'd had some really good ribs. While he couldn't chow down in the traditional sense, he could indulge in the flavorful aroma. A vampire's sense of smell was even more heightened—and much more satisfying—than a human's sense of taste. Which meant he could still enjoy the experience.

The sudden hankering certainly had nothing to do with the fact that Nikki was hungry and Jake wanted nothing more than to satisfy her every need. To see her full and content and happy.

Hell, no.

This was strictly sex.

"Lead the way," he told her. He was talking pure, rejuvenating, power-infusing sex. The woman had to keep up her strength.

9

"HOW HOT DO YOU WANT it, honey?" The question came from the middle-aged woman standing behind the counter at the barbecue stand. She wore a stained white apron and plastic gloves. Behind her, a silver drum-shaped pit gave off puffs of smoke. The smell of mesquite filled the air.

The woman held up the plate of prize-winning ribs Jake had just ordered and indicated the row of bottled sauces. "We got everything from Sissy Sauce to Hell, Fire & Brimstone," she added, "which, I have to tell you, ain't for weaklings." She pointed to a white piece of cardboard posted near a roll of paper towels. The sign warned against everything from mild indigestion to unwanted back hair.

Jake grinned and slid a gaze toward Nikki. His expression faded as he stared at her for several pulse-pounding moments. Then a teasing light fired his eyes and a grin tugged at the corner of his sensuous mouth. "I say the hotter, the better."

"Coming right up." Miss Myrna doused Jake's plate with enough sauce to eat through a sheet of cast iron. The spicy scent of Tabasco, chili pepper and jalapeño cut through the musky air and burned her nostrils.

At the same time, her mouth watered and she had the

sudden vision of herself licking a wayward dribble of sauce from Jake's chin. Her taste buds buzzed in anticipation.

She forced a smile. "No sauce for me."

"None?" Jake sounded incredulous as they took their plates and walked toward a cluster of picnic tables. "And here I thought you liked things blazing-hot."

"The ribs are fine on their own." She angled herself onto a nearby bench and set her plate in front of her.

Jake folded himself in across from her. His gaze locked with hers and those amazing silver eyes drilled into her. "Is that just a personal choice or is there an actual health concern that makes you antisauce?"

"Personal." She'd meant to stop at that. But he stared at her so intently—as if what she had to say really mattered to him—that she couldn't help herself. "My mom and I lived with my great aunt while I was growing up—my aunt Izzie. She's really sweet and she helped us out a lot."

"Where was your father?"

"He wasn't in the picture. My mother was sixteen when she had me. Alone. Unmarried. Her parents died in a car accident when she was really young and Aunt Izzie took her in. Anyhow, I grew up with them both, which wasn't very easy. They're polar opposites. Aunt Izzie's very stiff and proper and my mother isn't."

"And how does this relate to your barbecue sauce boycott?"

"My mother likes everything really spicy. She can eat her way through an entire bottle of Hell, Fire & Brimstone. Meanwhile, my great-aunt has a really sensitive digestive tract and she can't tolerate anything more than Sissy Sauce. We always had a bottle of each in our cupboard."

"And?"

"And if I used the Sissy Sauce, I had to hear it from my mother. And if I used the more potent stuff, I had to hear it from Aunt Izzie. No sauce, no argument."

"Sounds like the easy way out."

"You try eating dry ribs. So what about you?" she rushed on, eager to distract herself from the sudden urge to reach out and take a taste of his sauce. "Any dysfunctional relatives waiting at home?"

He shook his head. "I never knew my father. My mother tried to raise me, but she couldn't really take care of herself, much less me. When I was nine, I went to live with this couple who owned a nearby ranch."

"That was nice of them to take you in."

"I don't think nice had anything to do with it." His gaze brightened until Nikki could have sworn she saw a flash of red.

Red?

She blinked. His eyes faded into a rich, molten silver and she was left to wonder if maybe, just maybe, she hadn't inhaled too much mesquite smoke near the barbecue pits. "That must have been tough," she rushed on, eager to distract herself from the crazy thought. "Being away from your mother like that."

"I survived." She waited for him to elaborate, but he didn't.

"My mom and my aunt Izzie drive me crazy, but I don't know what I would do without them."

"I do." A knowing light gleamed in his eyes. "You

wouldn't be eyeballing my barbecue sauce. You'd be eating some." He held up his plate and challenge gleamed in his gaze. "You know you want a taste."

The scent wafted toward her and teased her nostrils. Before she could stop herself, she reached out and dipped her rib into the excess sauce. She brought the juicy bite to her lips. Taste exploded on her tongue, followed by a rush of fire that brought tears to her eyes.

"I should stick to the mild stuff," she murmured after she'd taken a long gulp of iced tea.

"You're still breathing. I'd say you handled it pretty well." A knowing light gleamed in his gaze and her heart stalled.

Her nipples tingled and she felt an aching throb between her legs. She wanted so much to dip her finger into the decadent sauce and rub it onto his sensuous mouth. Then touch her lips to his and sweep her tongue back and forth, tasting and nibbling and—

"Look," she rushed on, eager to kill the dangerous thought, "I know you probably think I'm pretty wild because of last night."

"And because of how fast you agreed to my counter offer tonight," he added, a grin tugging at his lips.

The expression eased her anxiety and she barely resisted the urge to smile. "I know how it looks, but I'm really not like that." She lowered her voice and leaned forward. "I don't usually sleep with someone outside of a relationship."

No way, no how was she going to fall into *like* with Jake McCann. Her mother had done that too many times to count, and she'd never managed to settle down. Not that she'd wanted to, of course. And so she'd fallen for men who hadn't been anything close to relationship material. They'd been good-looking. And only interested in sex. And very, very temporary.

Which described Jake McCann to the proverbial T.

His knee brushed hers under the table. Goose bumps chased up and down her skin. He didn't say anything as his gaze held hers, and she had the sudden urge to keep talking.

"Actually, I don't usually sleep with someone *in* a relationship. I mean, I have, but only after I've really gotten to know that person." She waited for him to say something, anything, but he simply looked at her, into her, as if seeing everything she'd yet to say. "Not that waiting did much good. The guys still turned out to be all wrong."

"Even this last guy? What was his name?"

Suddenly she couldn't seem to think of it. The only thing she could think of was how silver Jake's eyes were and how soft his lips had felt and how she really, *really* wanted to feel them again.

"Especially whatshisname," she rushed on before she could dwell too much on her sudden memory loss. "I didn't think so at first—but then, that's the story of my life. Meet a guy and get to know him before I sleep with him. Not that he and I slept together. Almost. But almost doesn't count. So you see, I'm really not like that."

He eyed her. "Like what, sugar?"

"You know. A bad girl."

A grin tugged at his lips. "There's nothing wrong with being a little bad every now and again."

If only.

She stifled the traitorous thought. She'd promised herself a long time ago that she wouldn't follow in her mother's footsteps—and she'd meant it. No hopping from one man to the next. No looking for love in all the wrong places. No ignoring everyone and everything in the process.

No rolling into work late, missing appointments, disappointing clients.

She stifled a sudden surge of guilt as she remembered that morning. She'd made a mistake. But Nikki learned from her mistakes and she wasn't going to let it happen again. She wasn't going to forget everything over a man—especially the wrong man.

"You build motorcycles, right?" she blurted, eager to fill up the sudden silence. Besides, the more she knew about him, the more she would realize that he was all wrong for her. "How did you get into that?"

He hesitated, and she couldn't help but think he was gauging just how much he wanted to tell her. "I've always loved to ride, but I couldn't really find a bike that I liked," he finally said. "So I decided to build my own."

"And?"

"I'd just finished when I ran into the editor for *Texas Chopper Magazine* at a local dealership where I'd gone to buy extra parts. He saw the bike and wanted to photograph it." He shrugged. "I let him. I didn't think anything about it. But the magazine got a flood of inquiries and, just like that, I was in business."

"What did you do before then?"

"Different things." His gaze locked with hers. "I've

herded cattle, nailed up Sheetrock, fixed transmissions." He shrugged. "I don't really like to be tied down."

"Does that go for your personal life, as well?"

"Especially my personal life."

"A commitmentphobe." She smiled despite the sudden disappointment that rolled through her.

"I prefer the term *confirmed bachelor.*" His mouth hinted at a grin.

She ignored her fluttering heart and concentrated on taking another bite of her food. "Same thing," she said after she'd swallowed. "Most commitmentphobes were either burned once and so they now avoid the big C or they're suffering from some hidden angst that makes them frightened of getting close to anyone for fear of discovery. So which is it with you?" She waved a rib at him. "Are you gun-shy or angsty?"

He sipped his iced tea and regarded her. "Does it matter?"

"Just curious." She narrowed her gaze and gave him a knowing look. "Of course, if you don't answer, then I'll assume you fall into the hidden-angst category because all hidden angsters don't want people to know they're screwed up. Hence the term *hidden.*"

"I thought you were a hairdresser, not a therapist."

"In a small town like Skull Creek, the two are synonymous. Same goes for bartenders." She shrugged. "It's okay if you don't feel comfortable coming out of the closet at this point." As soon as she made the statement, he frowned, and she couldn't help herself. "We really haven't known each other very long. Most of the men I've known wait until we've had at least a few more dates before they start acting weird—"

"I was married once," he cut in. "A long, long time ago. But it didn't work out."

"Why?" The question was out before she could stop herself.

He hesitated again, as if deciding how much he wanted to admit to her. Or to himself. "I had some problems…" He shook his head. "She couldn't deal with them and so she took off. That's it."

The sudden flicker of pain over his features sent a cattle prod straight to her heart. "I'm really sorry."

"Don't be." He shrugged. "Things were tough. *I* was tough. She did what she had to do. She found someone else and moved on."

"Did you hit her?"

Surprise flashed in his molten gaze. "Excuse me?"

"Did you hit her? Slap? Punch? Kick? Abuse her physically in any way shape or form?"

"*Hell,* no. I would never hurt a woman."

As if she didn't already know.

She did. While Jake stirred many feelings inside of her, fear wasn't one of them. The only thing Nikki feared was her reaction to him.

Fierce.

Overwhelming.

Addictive.

"What about mentally?" she prodded. "Were you controlling? Did you make her feel worthless? Unappreciated? Dumb? Fat?"

His initial outrage turned to amusement, as if the very idea was so far out of his realm of thought. "Hardly."

"How about her underwear? You didn't wear it, did you?"

A grin played at his lips. "I like peeling off women's undies, not wearing them."

As if she didn't already know.

Jake McCann had his own fetish. He was a bona fide sex maniac. Otherwise, he never would have made such an offer.

"What about her shoes?" she asked, eager to keep her mind on the topic rather than the anticipation that settled between her legs.

"They didn't fit."

"Her dresses?"

"Nope."

"Jewelry?"

"Nada."

"Then she shouldn't have betrayed you with another man. A promise is a promise. It's meant to be kept. That's why it says *for better or for worse*." She shook her head. "I'm never going to turn my back on someone I love. Ever." Her gaze met his. "Nobody deserves that."

"It doesn't matter." That's what Jake said. What he told himself as he stared across the table at Nikki and saw the certainty gleaming in her honey-colored eyes.

He'd long ago come to terms with what had happened. He'd been turned into a monster, for chrissake. Enslaved by evil, his body forever marked with the proof of that enslavement by the bands on his arms.

After that fateful night, Jake had camped out in the barn, sleeping all day and staying out all night. He'd been in denial then, living off the local livestock, frantically praying that the "sickness" would pass. Deep down, he'd known the truth, but he hadn't wanted to accept what had happened to him. And so he'd ignored it and tried to keep going. He'd worn long-sleeve shirts to conceal the marred skin of his arms. He'd grown reclusive, pale, sick.

Ellen had been more concerned with her own misery than his. She'd hitched a ride with a cowboy who'd been passing through town and left for good, and Jake had been glad.

For her sake.

Her father had followed. It had been the late 1800s, after all, and her father had been old-fashioned even for that day and age. He'd gone after her, determined to bring her back and mete out justice for the shame she'd caused him, and Jake had ridden in the opposite direction.

He'd been running ever since.

Nikki, for all her fancy words, would have up and left just like Ellen. Any woman would have. At the same time, with her staring so earnestly at him, sincerity gleaming in the intoxicating depths of her eyes, he could almost believe she meant what she said.

Not that he really cared one way or another. The past was the past and all that mattered now was the future.

The coming battle.

"Let's get out of here," he said, pushing to his feet.

"But you haven't even touched your food."

"I don't want food, sugar." His gaze caught and held hers. "I want you."

"LET'S TAKE A RIDE." Jake's deep voice slid into Nikki's ears as he pulled her to a stop in front of the Ferris wheel.

They were just shy of the carnival entrance, and with

every step Nikki's heart had beat that much faster. The frantic thump paused and took a nosedive straight into the murky depths of disappointment. "Now? But I thought... That is—" she glanced around at the crowd that moved around them "—I thought you wanted to get out of here."

"The point is to get in, darlin', not out." The serious expression that had carved his features earlier had faded and he'd lapsed into the charming Southern bad boy once again. "Besides, we've got all these tickets. Seems a shame to waste them, don't you think? Then again, you probably have a curfew." He winked. "What with you being such a good girl and all."

"I'm good but not that good."

"We'll see." Desire gleamed hot and bright in his gaze.

"But..." But nothing. This wasn't about the future, she reminded herself. It was about right now. The next few days. Which meant there was nothing wrong with letting her hair down and indulging her inner vixen.

For a little while.

"Let's ride," she told him.

"'Atta girl." He winked, and heat rushed through her body, firebombing every major erogenous zone along the way. Her cheeks heated, her nipples burned and the temperature between her legs spiraled to a dangerous level. It was a cool October night for Texas, yet she felt as if she were suddenly smack-dab in the middle of a sweltering summer.

Breathless. Anxious. *Bad.*

Jake guided her past the maze of ropes, toward the entrance to the ride.

"Hey, there, Nikki." The woman standing guard at the

entrance to the platform smiled before shifting her attention to Jake and the tickets he handed over.

"Hi, Willa. How's business at the bakery?" Willa Avery owned Sweet Eats and served as secretary for the chamber of commerce. She also volunteered for every chamber-sponsored event—in this case, the carnival—and kept the gossip flowing every Tuesday morning at the weekly meeting of the ladies' auxiliary.

"I can't complain." Her gaze roved over Jake. "I guess it's true. I heard you had a new boyfriend, but I didn't see as how it could be true." She spared a glance at Nikki. "What with it only being a few weeks since you and Bill split. Nikki isn't one to hop from boyfriend to boyfriend," she told Jake. "This whole thing seems too sudden, if you ask me."

"I've never been long on patience when it comes to something I want," Jake said. "I took one look and I knew she was the one. It was the same for Nikki here."

"Is that true?" Surprise swept Willa's face—not that Nikki could blame her. She'd spent her entire life proving to everyone that she wasn't her mother and she'd succeeded. Maybe a little too well.

"I wouldn't say it happened *that* fast. We knew each other before we decided to get involved." All of five seconds, she added silently.

"Really? How did you meet?"

"Hair convention," Nikki told her.

Willa's gaze swiveled to Jake. "You one of them models?"

"He's a stylist," Nikki blurted before Jake could reply. "He gives a mean perm. Don't you, honey?"

Willa's perplexed gaze shifted to Jake, who didn't look

the least bit happy about his new talent. Up on the platform, the Ferris wheel operator—a young man wearing a yellow Carnivals-R-Us shirt—unlocked the door of one of the cars, and a handful of giggling girls climbed out.

Nikki hooked her arm with his. "Don't be shy, honey. You know you're good."

"The best in Texas," he grunted as Nikki elbowed him.

"He means the second best," she told Willa. "Don't I have you scheduled next week?" Nikki asked as the operator unlocked and opened the next car. Another group of kids spilled out.

"Friday morning. Norman's taking me out for our anniversary and I want to look my best." Willa smiled. "He made reservations at my favorite restaurant and even booked us a room at one of them fancy hotels in Austin."

"Too sweet."

"He knows how to treat the woman who cooks him pot roast and new potatoes every Sunday. You'd do well to take a lesson from him, young man." She turned to Jake. "Nikki here is a nice girl, and you'd better treat her good." She wagged a finger at him. "No lying or cheating or borrowing her bikini panties. She's had enough of that to last her a lifetime."

"No worries there." Jake grinned. "I'm a brief man myself."

"Good for you." Willa motioned them toward the now-empty platform. "Have fun."

"We will," Jake murmured as he cupped Nikki's elbow and urged her up the steps. His lips grazed her earlobe and excitement rippled down her spine. "That's a promise."

10

NIKKI TRIED TO CALM her pounding heart as she settled on the vinyl-covered seat. Jake slid in next to her and pulled the bar across their laps until it locked into place.

She turned her head and tried to draw a deep breath that didn't smell of leather and hot, hunky male. She caught a whiff of candied apples and popcorn from a nearby concession stand, but the scents only served to make matters worse. Her stomach rumbled with renewed hunger and she damned herself for getting the ribs rather than something loaded with sugar. Jake sat too close, his thigh pressed firmly against hers, his scent teasing her nostrils, his strength surrounding her.

The closer, the better.

She drop-kicked the notion out as soon as it pushed its way in. While she might be looking forward to keeping her end of the bargain, she didn't intend to start here and now, in full view of everyone. What would they all think?

That she was every bit as wild and reckless as her mother had been. As irresponsible.

She wasn't. She might not be as upright as Aunt Izzie, but she wasn't like Jolene, either.

"You're not afraid of heights, are you?" Jake's deep voice slid into her ear and scrambled her thoughts.

"What makes you say that?"

"Because you're obviously afraid of something." He touched her trembling bottom lip, the rough pad of his finger cool against her skin. "It's either the ride or me, sugar."

Or me. "It's just a little indigestion. I ate too many ribs." When he didn't look convinced, she gave him a wide-eyed look. "Cross my heart." Before he could say anything more, the ride groaned into motion.

Jake slid one arm around her, his hand closing over one shoulder, and half turned. His free hand went to her thigh. Long, lean fingers caught the material of her skirt and pulled higher and higher, baring her knee, her thigh, until she felt his bare touch against the silky vee of her panties.

Her breath caught.

"Stop," she whispered and he did. He went stock-still, his fingertips burning through the thin material, stirring little shock waves that seemed to zap her fear.

"Is that what you really want?"

Yes. It was there on the tip of her tongue. A complete and totally irrational response considering she'd already made up her mind to do this—to let go of her inhibitions and indulge her inner bad girl until Jake McCann rolled out of town and out of her life.

At the same time, she'd been holding back for so long that she wasn't sure if she could really and truly do this. No holds barred. *Wild.*

"I've never…" She licked her lips. "That is, I don't usually do things like this."

"You say that like it's a bad thing."

"It is in this situation. You're probably used to really experienced women, and I'm not. I know all the basics, but I'm no expert. I've never had sex in the backseat of a car or in a department store dressing room. I'm not a member of the Mile High club. I've never even licked chocolate body paint off of anyone." Her gaze locked with his. "And I've certainly never had sex on a carnival ride."

His grin was slow and easy and completely disarming. "Who said anything about sex?" His expression grew dark and serious and hungry. "This isn't about the main event, sugar. It's about the buildup. About stirring the excitement until you can't take it anymore." He leaned in and touched his lips to hers. It wasn't really a kiss. Not really. Just the faintest press of his mouth and the unspoken promise of more. Her heart skipped its next beat and every nerve in her body buzzed in anticipation.

Maybe it was the way he looked at her—as if he'd never seen a woman as beautiful or that he wanted as much—or maybe it was the fact that she'd never seen a man so beautiful or that she wanted so much. Maybe a little of both. But just like that her inhibitions seemed to slip away, and suddenly the only thing that mattered was that he *didn't* stop touching her.

As if he read the thoughts racing through her mind, his hand dropped to her knee again and slid up the inside of her thigh. Slow. So enticingly slow. Her breath caught.

"I thought you were a brief man," she breathed as his finger hooked the edge of her panties. She shifted as he tugged, and the silky fabric slid down her thighs and over her knees.

"I lied." His fingertips grazed her ankles as he pulled the undies free and stuffed them into his jeans pocket.

"You don't wear women's underwear."

He grinned. "And now neither do you."

A twinge of embarrassment went through her as cool air ruffled under her skirt to tease her bare flesh.

"Seriously, what are you going to do with them?"

"The question is, what are you going to do without them?" Before she could answer, Jake's fingers swept up the inside of her thigh and stirred a slow-burning heat that started at the tips of her toes and spread north.

He trailed his touch up the inside of her thigh, coming close to the heat between her legs—but not too close. Just enough to stall the air in her lungs and make her want to reach down, take his hand and show him exactly where and how deep she wanted to feel him.

She was about to do just that when the ride started to slow. Over. *Finally.*

That's what she told herself, but she didn't feel the expected relief. Instead her body burned and her legs trembled and it was all she could do to follow Jake from the car and not jump his bones right there on the spot.

As if he sensed her urgency, he handed off the rest of their tickets to a group of kids and headed for the parking lot.

"Want to drive?" he asked her when they reached his motorcycle.

She almost shook her head. Old habits died hard and

Nikki had been denying her wild side far too long to stop just like that.

Eight days, she reminded herself. "Why not? I've always wondered what it would be like to drive one of these things."

"This, sugar, is not a *thing*." One large hand trailed over the handlebars in a loving, reverent caress that she actually felt down the length of her own spine. "It's a one-of-a-kind with custom aluminum rims, handcrafted leather trim and an 1100cc engine. It's sleek and fast and you'll never see another like it." His narrowed gaze swept her flushed face. "Are you sure you're not too distracted?"

"No." His warm chuckle vibrated along her nerve endings. "But what the hell? Let's give it a shot anyway." She glanced at the black-and-chrome motorcycle. Her adrenaline pumped and her pulse raced.

"After you." He motioned for her to get on and he climbed behind her.

She was a quick study. In five minutes they were pulling out of the gravel lot and rounding the high school. In ten they were zooming down the main farm road, headed out of town.

Nikki tightened her grip on the handlebars and tried to ignore the awareness that gripped her. The wind whipped at her face and teased the edges of her skirt, whipping the material back and forth in a sharp motion against her thighs. Jake's powerful legs framed hers, his chest a solid wall of muscle against her shoulder blades. One sinewy arm held her tightly around the waist while the other supported her grip on the handlebars, his fingers warm atop hers.

"You're doing great. A little old-ladyish for my tastes, but it'll do." His deep voice slid into her ears. She wouldn't have heard him over the rush of wind, but he was close, his lips grazing her ear.

"Gee, you really know how to sweet-talk a girl."

"I've never been much of a talker." His lips grazed her ear again. "I usually let my actions speak for me." His arm eased around her waist and his hand slid between her legs.

Nikki's breath caught, her grip faltered and the bike swerved.

"Watch it." He caught the handlebars with both hands, his arms on either side of her as he helped her regain her grip. "You have to keep your mind on the road."

"Easy for you to say." She tightened her grip beneath his and held the bike steady. "You've still got your underwear on."

Laughter rumbled in her ears and thrummed through her senses. "Who says I'm wearing any?"

The question made her keenly aware of the hardness pressing against her buttocks.

"I'm sorry this is such a difficult situation for you." His hands fell away, his palms resting on the muscular thighs that flanked hers. "But it could be worse."

"Oh, really? How's that?"

"Well…" The word was a slow, deep drawl. "I could be touching you right now, sliding my fingers into your slick flesh, plunging deep…" His tongue flicked her ear.

Her grip on the gas faltered and the motorcycle jerked. "Maybe you should drive," she said as his hands took control, "before we end up in the nearest ditch."

"What the lady wants, the lady gets." He urged the bike even faster. The wheels ate up gravel as they flew at a steady, smooth pace that said Jake McCann was used to being in control and going fast. Very fast.

"You're a really good driver," she called out.

"It's all in the hands, darlin'. All in the hands." To emphasize his point, he released his grip on one of the handlebars and let his touch fall to her bare knee. "See, some bikers like to use their thighs to control the machine, but I think a soft but steady touch at just the right spot—" his fingers splayed against her flesh and slid toward the inside of her knee "—works much better." He caught the edge of her skirt and pushed it up. "See, motorcycles aren't that much different from people. They'll do just what you want if you know how to stroke them. If you want a nice, slow, leisurely ride, you keep your touch loose, not too much pressure." His fingers made lazy circles on the inside of her thigh and a dizzying heat rushed through Nikki.

"You want a fast, hard ride, you tighten your grip and exert more pressure." His fingers swept higher, his touch more intense as he moved beneath the edge of her skirt and higher until he was a scant inch shy of the slick folds between her legs. "See the difference?"

Boy, could she ever. Slow. Fast. She wasn't sure which one she liked more. They'd both sent her spiraling toward the land of gaga. She licked her lips and tried to form an intelligent reply.

"Yes," she managed. "Big difference."

"So what's your personal preference? Slow? Fast?"

"Now."

His chest vibrated behind her and the deep rumble of

laughter filled her ears. "That's not a choice, sugar. But I think I can help you out." His thumb brushed the slick folds between her legs and sensation speared, hot and jagged, through her already trembling body.

"You're so wet." The words were more of a groan. "So warm and wet and…" His voice faded into the buzz of wind and excitement that filled her ears.

She tilted her head back, resting it in the curve of his shoulder as she gave over to the ecstasy beating at her sanity and let him take control—of her aching body.

He slid a finger inside her and the air bolted from her lungs. He moved and she did, too, shifting just so, drawing him deeper, riding his fingers the way the two of them rode the powerful machine.

He knew just how to touch her, how to push himself deep until the air lodged in her throat and her senses flooded with sensation. When she knew she couldn't take any more, he withdrew just enough to let her catch her breath. Stroke. Plunge. Withdraw.

He seemed to touch her everywhere, as if he used both hands instead of one. The sensation too intense. Too consuming. Of course, that was crazy. That's what she told herself, but her eyes flicked open anyway.

Her gaze zigzagged from one hand grip to the other. The bike held steady, screaming forward while Jake held her with both hands, teased her, drove her to the brink of the most exquisite orgasm.

No. Her eyes snapped shut. This couldn't be happening. Could it?

Before the question plagued her, Jake slid a second

finger deep inside, and just like that she came apart in his arms. Shudders vibrated through her body, skimming along her ragged senses in wave after wave of sweet, decadent sensation.

She slumped back against him, weak and damp, her breath raspy, her heartbeat a frenzied rhythm in her chest. By the time she managed to force her eyes open again Jake had both hands firmly on the handlebars.

As if he'd never let go in the first place. He hadn't. He couldn't have. They would have crashed into the nearest tree.

Then again, maybe he'd built some special navigation controls into the bike. Sort of like the autopilot on an airplane.

Not that she'd ever heard of such a thing, but maybe he was blazing new innovative trails in motorcycle engineering.

Probably.

That or…or what? He was some superhero with special mind control powers?

There was no *or*. He'd built a tricked-out navigation system. End of story.

Filing away the thought, she turned her attention to the real matter at hand—breathing again. She drew deep draughts of air, in and out, as Jake turned the bike around and headed back to town.

The ride was too long and too stirring with Jake surrounding her and the bike vibrating between her legs. By the time they pulled up in front of the familiar yellow bungalows with the matching picket fence, she was more than ready for more.

But not here.

This place…this was her future. The first step toward her happily ever after.

"The motel," she blurted, because tonight wasn't part of Nikki's happily ever after, even if she did have a sudden unsettling vision of Jake carrying her over the threshold. "I just moved in and I'm in the middle of remodeling. Everything's a mess. You still have a room, don't you?"

He stiffened, and she thought he might climb off, sweep her into his arms and head for the front door regardless of her hesitation. Her heart pounded once, twice, but then his deep voice slid into her ears. "I've got the room for the week."

"Good. Let's go there." Relief swept her as he kicked the bike back to life and circled back around.

It was late and the Skull Creek Inn was dark except for the Vacancy sign that buzzed out front. He climbed off the bike, pulled her after him and headed for the stairs.

A few seconds later, he pulled her inside his room, slammed and locked the door and hauled her flush against his body. His mouth covered hers, his lips plundering in a kiss that made her so wet she could actually feel the trickle of moisture along the inside of her thigh.

He backed her up against the nearest wall, flat against the window. His palms flattened against the glass, his arms braced on either side. He dipped his head, his tongue claiming hers in a deep, wet kiss. Then he licked his way down the side of her neck. Her pulse jumped, thudding through her veins.

KA-THUNK, KA-THUNK, *ka-thunk.*

Her pulse beat a mesmerizing tempo that stirred his

hunger, and drew him even more than the delicious heat seeping from her body.

Sex, he reminded himself. Jake had fed just last night. He shouldn't be hungry yet.

He wasn't, he reminded himself. Not yet.

He forced his mouth lower, to the vee of her blouse. His fingers made quick work of its buttons until he parted the material, unsnapped her bra and shoved aside the lacy cups. Then his hot mouth closed over one rose-colored nipple and a moan parted her lips.

He teased the ripe peak with his tongue, laving and stroking. And then he sucked her in, drawing so long and deep that a shudder vibrated through her body. She was so close to the edge. *Again.*

The realization hit Jake hard and fast, like a sucker punch that came from out of nowhere, and stunned him for a long moment.

No fuckin' way could she be gearing up for another orgasm. Not when the first had been so intense, so powerful, so draining.

The rush of energy had been full force, like an electrical surge from the point of contact, throughout his body. He'd felt the power fill him up, and then she'd collapsed against him.

Yet here she was ready for more. For him.

He could feel it in the tremble of her ripe body, see it in the desperation that turned her eyes a deep, rich, vibrant gold. He heard it in the short raspiness of her breaths. He smelled it, too, the sweet, heady aroma of a sexy, aroused, hungry woman.

His own hunger stirred again, an ache that roared to full, throbbing awareness as he suckled her. Her pulse beat echoed in his ears, exciting him all the more, making him want to take more than the sex.

But he wouldn't just be taking then. No, he would be giving back, forging an unbreakable bond with her. One that he wouldn't be able to walk away from if he failed to reclaim his humanity.

Urgency rushed through him and he suckled her harder. Her body bowed, arching into him, offering everything he desperately wanted to take.

Everything.

Her throat gleamed pale and white in the moonlight and his insides tightened. A shudder went through his body and a groan rumbled up his throat. His eyes opened and he caught his reflection in the window. Two pinpoints of bright violet light gleamed back at him.

Proof of his desire.

Proof that he was anything but the man she thought him to be.

"Jake?" His name slipped from her lips and her eyelids fluttered. Before she could fully open them, he whirled her around until she faced the glass and her sweet ass strained against the hard bulge in his pants.

"I need to be inside of you," he rasped, nuzzling her ear. He slid his arms around her and caught her nipples. He plucked and played until the tender tips swelled and hardened and she gasped.

His hands fell to her thighs. His fingers bunched the fabric of her skirt until he touched bare skin. He made quick work of his own zipper, shoving the denim down his hips until his erection bobbed forward, pressing into the soft flesh of her bottom.

Now, a voice whispered. *Take her now!*

But he couldn't...he wouldn't....He wasn't sure how he managed to hold back until he'd pulled a ~~condom~~ from his pocket, but he did.

"I'll help," she offered, but he wasn't about to take the risk. For whatever reason, Nikki pushed him to the edge when it came to control.

But she didn't send him spiraling over. Not yet.

"I've got it." ~~He opened the packet,~~ sheathed himself and pressed her back up against the wall. He flattened one palm against the wall and locked an arm around her waist to anchor her for a full upward thrust.

The blood drummed so loudly in his ears he barely heard her gasp of pleasure, her sob for more. Her body was warm and ripe, clenching and unclenching around him even though they were both standing so perfectly still.

For several deep, shallow breaths he just stood there, relishing the delicious energy that buzzed and whirled in her lush body. When she came apart, the energy would transfer, rushing through every point of contact, drenching his muscles, fueling his senses until he felt empowered. *Alive*.

He began to move, sliding his cock deep into her warmth, only to withdraw. In. Out. Pleasure splintered his brain with each furious thrust distracting him from the gnawing in his belly. The heat grew hotter, bolder, drawing him in until he pumped faster. Harder. *Oh, man*.

She came first, crying his name as violent tremors

racked her body. The surge of energy rushed at him, crashing over him like a tidal wave and sucking him under. He came then, bucking and spilling himself deep inside as he held her tight.

He scooped her up into his arms and dropped them both down onto the bed. The moonlight pushed through the open windows, bathing them in a warm, celestial glow. It was the warmest he'd ever felt at night. And the most content. And he liked it.

He liked her.

Of course you like her. She's juicing you up for the big confrontation.

But there was more to it than that. It wasn't just the whirlwind of energy that drew him to her, it was the feelings. The sincerity in her gaze when she'd talked about making promises. The conviction when she'd talked about keeping them. She was caught between her mother and her aunt, yet she loved them both. Enough to forfeit her own happiness and try to please each of them.

That's what she was doing.

He recognized it because he'd spent his entire life trying to please everyone else. First his mother. Then Mr. Caskey. Then Ellen and her father. Then the damnable hunger.

Jake's entire world now revolved around lust. The lust for sex. For blood. For revenge. For his own humanity. Rarely did he feel anything else. But when he'd sat at the picnic table with Nikki, he'd felt an overwhelming sense of camaraderie. And compassion. And understanding.

For those few precious moments he'd felt like a man.

Her man.

He gathered her close and relished the feel of her soft skin against his own, and for the first time he let himself imagine what things might be like if the situation were different.

If *he* were different.

Maybe he wouldn't walk away when all was said and done. Maybe, just maybe, he would actually settle down right here. With Nikki.

If.

11

IT WAS ALMOST OVER.

Nikki ate her last bite of waffle and downed the remaining sip of juice. She'd arrived at the ancient farmhouse where she'd spent her childhood a good half hour ahead of her mother, who'd overslept thanks to another late night.

Not Nikki. She'd been early.

No sleeping an extra three hours or trying to sneak in another spectacular orgasm. She'd scrambled out of bed around four o'clock. and left Jake sound asleep. She had things to do and places to go, a routine, and she'd been determined to keep her priorities straight.

Once home, she'd done what she did every Sunday morning—she'd watched the last episode of *Grey's Anatomy* on Tivo. Then she'd ordered some salon supplies on-line and put together the ad she was going to run in Tuesday's paper—complete with a Fall Ball discount coupon. She'd also hung up the various paint swatches in her kitchen and tried to decide which colors she liked best. Then she'd put on her Sunday best and now she was here.

She eyed the empty plate and smiled.

Yep, the inquisition would end soon.

"Here, dear." Izzie wore an apron decorated with

bright pink pigs, her favorite peach colored skirt set and a warm smile. "Have another blueberry waffle before we leave for church."

"Leave the poor girl alone, Aunt Izzie." Jolene sat across from Nikki, her gaze hooked on the latest issue of *Cosmo*. She wore a hot-pink peasant blouse and a colorful Mexican skirt. Her hair was combed and teased to blonde perfection, her makeup firmly in place. "She's already had two. You're going to make her fat."

"She could stand to have a little meat on her bones." Izzie plopped down another waffle on Nikki's plate.

"No man's going to want her if she balloons up like a blimp." Jolene grabbed the edge of the plate and handed it back to the old woman.

"She already has a man who loves her for better or worse." Izzie set the waffle in front of Nikki again.

"She's not marrying him." Jolene handed the plate back.

"She most certainly is." Izzie set the plate down again.

"I'll eat half." Nikki held her arms protectively around the plate and grabbed her fork.

"So when can we meet this young man?" Izzie asked again, for probably the dozenth time since Nikki had walked through the front door. She'd first replied, "Soon," but Izzie seemed determined to wrangle a definite answer from her.

The last thing she wanted was to introduce Jake to her great-aunt. With his good looks and charisma, Izzie would surely fall in love with him, and that would only make fading him out of the picture that much more difficult.

"There's no reason to meet him," Jolene said. "They're not getting married."

"Yes, they are."

"No, they're not—"

"What are you reading, Mom?" Nikki blurted, eager to change the subject.

"An article about Texas bachelors. It says here that Dallas has more doctors and lawyers and financial gurus than any other city in Texas. Of course, they don't have much to offer by way of construction workers or the more rugged types. If you want to meet a cowboy, you have to drive to Austin. Or Midland. Midland's got lots of cowboys."

"How about insurance agents?" Aunt Izzie settled down at the table with her own plate of waffles.

"Who wants to date an insurance agent?" Jolene sipped her coffee. "I'm talking about men who've amounted to something. Sports stars, entertainers, Internet traders, real-estate gurus."

"An insurance agent is something." Namely because Aunt Izzie's one and only true love had once been an insurance agent named Tom. He'd gotten hit by a truck before they'd married, and Aunt Izzie had mourned him ever since.

"I like insurance agents myself," Nikki offered. "William over at the State Farm office is pretty hot."

"He barely makes enough money to buy those hideous suits that he wears," Jolene said.

"They do look a little dated," Nikki agreed.

"Vintage," Izzie quipped. "Isn't that what you young people call it?"

"It's only vintage if it's done on purpose," Jolene told Izzie. "If you're just wearing it because it's all you have, then it's just plain old."

"Maybe it's all he has," Nikki offered. She cut half the waffle into four pieces and shoved one into her mouth.

One down...three to go.

"He's the top-rated agent in town," Jolene went on. "He makes plenty of money, he just doesn't want to part with any of it. He's cheap."

"There's nothing wrong with being thrifty," Izzie said. "I'm thrifty."

"My point exactly. Look at this place, Iz. You've got the same wallpaper that you had back in the fifties—"

"What about your date last night?" Nikki cut in, drawing her mother's attention. "Who was he?" She stuffed bite number two into her mouth and chewed.

"Bernie Maguire." A smile touched Jolene's lips. "The man is a total dreamboat."

Nikki tried to reconcile the Bernie she knew with the *dreamboat* concept. He was fifty-something, three times divorced, no kids, with a fake tan and dyed hair. He wore his pants too tight and enough gold chains to feed a family of four for the next fifty years.

"We went for a steak dinner over at Olsen's Diner—he had a rib eye while I had my usual salad—and then we went two-stepping over at this new dance hall in Calloway."

Nikki shoved bite number three into her mouth.

"I heard about that place," Izzie said. "They were raided last month by the sheriff's office for selling drugs."

"They did not get raided. One of the deputies was having a bachelor party and the whole lot of them showed up to wish him well."

Nikki forked the last piece.

"That's not what Amelia Patterson said," Izzie pointed out.

Chew.

"Amelia Patterson is almost one hundred years old," Jolene countered. "She can barely stay awake during bingo."

Swallow.

"She stays awake most of the time."

"Why, she hasn't kept her eyes open for more than—"

"Done," Nikki announced. She pushed back from the table. "I hate to eat and run, but I really have to go."

"What about church?" Izzie asked.

Nikki thought about two hours sandwiched between Izzie and Winona—Jolene didn't *do* church—and shook her head. " I need to run by the hardware store before I head over to the senior's center." She volunteered her hairstyling services every Sunday to the Greyhounds who couldn't afford an actual salon visit.

"Such dedication." Izzie beamed. "Let me fix you a snack to take with you."

"Stop stuffing the girl." Jolene stood. "You're going to make her sick."

"It's just a little something to tuck into her bag for later."

Nikki opened her mouth to referee, but her brain had snagged on the word *bag*. As in the black leather satchel she used to carry around her hair supplies.

Dread bubbled as her mind raced back through the past few hours. She'd been so anxious to keep up her usual routine and not let herself get distracted that she'd done just that. She'd gone off and left her bag—filled with everything from her scissors to her combs to her mother's favorite hair conditioner—sitting on the kitchen table.

"Here you go, dear." Izzie handed her a stuffed brown paper sack. "Have a nice day."

But Nikki's day had already been shot to hell.

She'd *forgotten*.

To make matters worse, she now had to drive back home and pick up her bag, which meant she couldn't stop by the hardware store without being late to Golden Acres. Which meant she'd let Jake McCann screw up her schedule.

Again.

"LET'S SEE WHAT YOU got."

Jake stared at the two aces and three kings he held in his hands and fanned them out on the table, a smile on his face as he stared at the man seated across from him. "Let's see you beat this."

The man took one look, threw down his own hand and muttered a curse.

"How about we go double or nothing?" Jake shoved the stack of gold coins he'd won toward the center of the table. "I'll even spot you a couple of cards."

"It's too damned late for me," the man muttered. "Besides, I intend to walk away with my britches on, and right now that's about all I have left."

"What about you?" Jake's gaze went to the next man.

Hopkins, who owned the general store across the street, shook his head and pushed away. "Got me a sweet little filly waitin' upstairs and I ain't of a mind to piss her off."

"Willy?" Jake eyed the owner of the livery stable.

"I'm out, too."

"That's what I get for playing with amateurs." Jake had wiped out a table of professionals just last week, a match that had ended with him having to draw his gun. They hadn't taken too kindly to losing to a local and so they'd been sore losers. And damned dangerous ones.

"It's late." Willy shrugged. *"I promised the wife I wouldn't be late again. I already missed supper twice this week. You ought to head on out, too. Ellen's probably waiting."*

Not yet. Her daddy liked to eat late—after he'd taken an evening nap—and so she was just cooking supper at this point. Liver and onions. Her daddy's favorite. But Jake wasn't her daddy and he couldn't stomach liver and onions. Any more than he could stomach the cold, hard man who'd forced him to marry his daughter because he'd caught Jake compromising her virtue.

Truth be told, Ellen's virtue had been compromised a helluva long time before Jake had hooked up with her. But he'd been the one who'd gotten caught. The one her father had wanted—needed—to help with his horses. The one who'd been so naive and love-struck that he'd actually believed Ellen had felt something for him.

She hadn't. He'd been headed out of town—free for the first time in his life—and she'd wanted to go with him. And so she'd done everything she could to make him want to take her along.

She'd lied to him. She hadn't been the least bit in love with him. Rather, she'd wanted out. Out of this town. Away from her domineering father.

Instead she was stuck.

They both were.

He gathered up his gold, downed the last of his whiskey and reached for his hat. Outside, he stepped down off the porch and stared toward the livery, where he'd left his horse.

Music drifted from the far end of the street, and Jake thought of the sizable amount he'd won tonight. Enough to take off for good if he'd been the kind to turn his back on a promise.

That or he could buy Ellen that dress she'd been wanting from that fancy-schmancy mail-order catalog.

She'd like that. And maybe, just maybe, she'd like him. For a little while anyhow.

He turned toward the saloon. A few more games, he told himself. Three at the most, and then he would head home.

Because Jake McCann kept his promises. He always had and he always would.

By the time he walked out of Mattie's, it was well after midnight. On his third round he'd wiped out a group of ranch hands from one of the neighboring farms, and they were none too happy. It was time to get while the getting was good.

He stepped down off the porch and started for the livery stable. Mud squished beneath his boots. The street stretched out in front of him, so dark and quiet.

Too quiet.

Even so, Jake didn't hear so much as a footfall behind him before he felt the hand close around his throat.

White-hot pain ripped through his jugular and blood gushed down the front of his shirt. A growl ripped open the silence. Jake felt the mouth at his neck, drawing on the open gash, sucking the life right out of him.

"No!"

The grip on his throat disappeared and Jake slumped to the ground. The sound of his heart beat a slow, sluggish rhythm in his ears, each ka-thump *growing further and further apart as he lay there for what seemed like an eternity. He was dying. He knew it, but there wasn't a damned thing he could do about it.*

He tried to keep his eyes open, to call for help, to offer up his winnings in exchange for his life, but the only sound that came out was a choked gurgle.

"You can't die." The tortured voice pushed past the pain thundering in Jake's head and he felt his body being lifted.

Help. Someone was helping him.

He wasn't sure what happened next because the pain overwhelmed him. By the time it calmed enough for him to actually breathe, he was lying on a soft bed of straw.

The scent of hay mingled with the musky aroma of animal hair. A barn. Maybe. He couldn't tell because there were none of the usual sounds. Just an eerie quiet and the occasional whistle of the wind. And something else.

A presence.

He fought for a breath and forced his eyes open. Through a blurry haze he saw the dark shadow of a man leaning over him. A knife glittered in a sliver of moonlight that pushed through the gaps in the roof.

Jake fixed his gaze on the curved blade, desperate to focus, to see the markings that had been cut into the sharp steel. Sam Black. *The letters gleamed as they caught another shaft of moonlight. Blood coated the hands that held the knife. Jake blinked again, but he'd seen enough. This was the man who'd tried to kill him.*

The man who was about to finish the job.

Jake struggled, but he couldn't make his arms and legs cooperate. The shadow raised the knife and sliced it through the air. Jake waited for the pain. More blinding pain. But it didn't come this time. Instead the blade sliced into the muscular forearm of the man who held it and drew a thin line of red blood.

"You have to drink," a deep, raspy voice urged. "Before it's too late."

Jake fought as the red heat splashed into his mouth and pushed at the man's bleeding arm. But the blood kept coming and coming, filling his mouth, running over his chin to glide down his throat and mingle with his own.

He sputtered and choked and then it was simply too much. He closed his eyes and gave up the fight.

He felt his body being rolled into a coarse blanket and then a weight pushed down on him as if he were being buried.

But he wasn't dead yet. Not completely. His heart still beat. Once. Twice. He heard it. He felt it.

And then he stopped feeling altogether.

Dead...

Jake bolted to a sitting position. His chest heaved and his pulse raced. He stared at the dark emptiness of the cave that surrounded him. In the far distance he heard the buzz of crickets. It was barely sunset and he should still be sleeping the sleep of the dead.

But he wasn't.

He closed his eyes and thought about the day after the attack. He'd found himself buried beneath a pile of hay in an abandoned barn miles from Junction. He'd been frantic, clutching at his chest, only to find that it hadn't been ripped to shreds.

A dream.

That's what he'd thought at first. That the attack had been a weird, twisted nightmare courtesy of the bottle of whiskey he'd nursed while playing his last round of cards. But deep down, deep down, he'd known the truth. Even before the first pangs of hunger had hit him. For sex. For blood....

He'd been dead, all right. And reborn at the same time. No longer a man but a vampire.

And vampires didn't have nightmares when they slept. They rested, rejuvenated, healed. It was all-consuming. There was no waking up for a snack. No tossing and turning. No thoughts of any kind. No dreams like the one he'd just had.

Jake blinked and rubbed a hand over the left side of his chest. Muscles rippled beneath his touch, his skin as smooth, as perfect as always. He touched his lips. Sure enough, there was no blood. Still, he could taste it. He could taste *him*.

He was close.

That's why Jake had had the dream. There was no doubt now that the Sam Black they'd written about on the plaque in the town park was the same one that had turned Jake. Sam had died here and so he was on his way, heeding the call the way they all did.

Jake could feel it in the awareness that rippled through his body and the vivid memories that rushed through him. Sam was close, all right.

Too close.

And?

And nothing. It was what Jake had been waiting for, expecting, and so he shouldn't have been the least bit freaked out. He was supposed to be celebrating.

Jake pushed to his feet, dove into the warm spring water and spent the next ten minutes determined to wash away his uneasiness.

When he was done, he climbed from the water, dropped to his sleeping bag and stretched out. He still had a good hour until sunset. He should try to sleep a little longer. He needed to sleep.

At the same time, he couldn't shut out the images that popped into his head. The shadow. The knife. Nikki.

Her image slipped into his thoughts and he saw her the way she'd been last night—under him, surrounding him, her expression blissful as she came apart in his arms.

Suddenly the image shifted and she stood in her salon. She wore the same white blouse and black skirt she'd worn yesterday. He watched as she stood at the cash register counting out money, a Closed sign on the front door. She'd just rubber-banded a stack of fives when a hand seemed to come from nowhere and glide around her throat and—

Jake opened his eyes, killing the image. He scrubbed a hand over his face and sat up.

Shit. He was going off the deep end. First he couldn't

sleep and now he was imagining Nikki facing the same situation he'd faced.

She wouldn't. Vampires were few and far between and there were none—besides himself—in Skull Creek.

Not yet, anyway.

Even when Sam arrived, he wouldn't get a chance to hurt anybody. Jake would take him out too fast. Clean and swift and *dead*.

And then Jake would be free.

He pulled on his jeans and a T-shirt and stepped into his boots. Climbing onto his bike, he kicked the engine to life and hauled ass into town to see Nikki.

The sex, he told himself as he maneuvered through the trees toward the main road. With Sam so close, Jake needed all the power he could get. And fast. The plaque, not to mention Jake's research, listed the date of death seven days from now. Which meant at midnight, when next Sunday rolled into Monday, Sam would revisit the exact spot where he'd turned. Jake had to soak up as much energy as possible before then.

His sudden anxiety certainly had nothing to do with the fierce surge of protectiveness that swamped him every time he thought about someone hurting her.

12

"So what do you think of my new eyebrows?"

Nikki stood in the recreation room at Golden Acres and stared at the bright red arches that had been carefully tattooed above Eula Holly's eyes.

Eula was in her nineties, a small woman with dyed red hair and frosted orange lipstick. Back in the day, Eula had been named Miss October at the Fall Ball five years in a row. Now she spent her time knitting and playing dominoes with her twin sister, Beula. She and Beula shared a room, as well as the same shade of lipstick, and they were always the first customers in line when Nikki made her weekly stop at the retirement home.

"I saw it in one of them fashion magazines and so's I had it done yesterday when we took our weekly field trip to Austin for lunch and shopping." She held up her bony fingers, which trembled ever so slightly. "My hands were starting to shake so bad when I tried to pencil them in that I figured this would save me a lot of trouble."

"And doctor bills," Beula, just as small with the same shade of hair, added. "Eula here stabbed herself in the eye two weeks ago. And the week before that she stabbed herself in the ear." Beula shrugged, "Who knew her aim could be that off?"

"Ronald Dupree came up behind me and scared the bejesus out of me, that's all," Eula said defensively.

"You're just getting old," Beula told her. "We all are. That's why we're here."

Because they were old. And because most had been forgotten. There were a few who received the dutiful visits from sons and daughters and grandchildren. But most of the residents at Golden Acres were there because they had nowhere else—and no one else who cared one way or another.

Eula and Beula weren't that much older than Nikki's aunt Izzie. In fact, they played bingo with her every Saturday night.

Not that Izzie would ever be forgotten. When the time came, Nikki would be there for Izzie the way Izzie had been there for her.

And Jolene?

Jolene would be there, too. She seemed almost heartless at times, but she wasn't. She was simply spoiled.

"You might be this side of giving up the ghost, but I'm not," Eula went on, distracting Nikki from her thoughts. "I'm still as spry as ever." Her hand trembled and she caught it with her other and held them in her lap. "I *am*," she said as if to convince herself more than Nikki. "So what do you think? They look perfect to me."

"That's 'cause you cain't see two inches in front of your face," Beula chimed in. "You need to wear your glasses."

"I do not need to wear glasses. Those are just for reading."

"The doctor said to wear them all the time."

"What does he know? The last time I was at his office, he was two hours late for my appointment. Probably out running around with God knows who."

"You were two hours early on account of you can't see the dadburned clock."

"I can see just fine."

"When you're wearing your glasses," Beula pointed out. "Tell her, would ya, Nikki? She's as blind as an old bat."

Nikki surveyed the eyebrows which were, hands down, about three shades too bright for the old woman's deep red hair color.

Nikki chose her words carefully. "It might be a good idea to wear your glasses a little more often." When Eula looked ready to tear up she added, "Not that the color's off. It's just that you look really nice in glasses. They make your eyes seem bigger and brighter."

"They do?"

"Absolutely. As for the eyebrows…" She studied the woman's hair for a long second. "I've been thinking that we should lighten you up a little, maybe add a few high-lights. If we do that, the eyebrows will be perfect." Or at least close enough for Eula not to be embarrassed. Nikki gave the older woman an encouraging smile. "I bet that's what you were thinking when you had the eyebrows done, wasn't it? Talk about intuitive."

"It was?" As if Nikki's meaning seemed to sink in, she nodded. "Yep, that's right. That's exactly what I was thinking. See there, Beula? I was right on the money when I asked for this color."

"Harrumph," Beula snorted. "Let's hope your intuition

holds up later when it really counts. You're playing tonight, aren't you, Nikki? The girls and I saved a spot for you."

Nikki nodded toward her purse. "I'm armed and ready."

She spent the next hour giving Eula highlights. After that, she did a set and roll on Beula, perms on Mrs. Hargrove and Mrs. Weatherspoon, three more colors and then a cut and blow-dry on Mr. Crabtree.

Being at Golden Acres every Sunday afternoon was like watching a CNN marathon. She heard about everything from a shooting in Detroit to a man caught flashing himself during a NASCAR race in California to the latest controversy going on in the retirement home's cafeteria.

"So I told everyone you've got to have the tapioca on account of some people are allergic to chocolate and it just ain't right to alienate good folks on account of they have delicate digestive systems," Mr. Crabtree said, his expression serious.

"Couldn't you just serve tapioca and chocolate cake and let everyone pick their poison?"

"The cook will only make one dessert per night. And she ain't even inclined to do that after those busybodies in the knitting circle passed around a petition trying to get her ousted on account of they said she was being uncooperative. You'd be uncooperative, too, if you had a bunch of know-it-alls telling you how to do your job." Mr. Crabtree leaned closer to the mirror. "I think you might have missed a spot right here."

"Really? Let me fix that." She pretended to snip off a few wayward hairs. "There. All done."

"If you ask me, the world's goin' to hell pretty damned fast."

"Just because the knitting circle wants chocolate cake? Maybe they just like chocolate. I've got a weakness for Milky Ways myself."

"Why, not a one of those old biddies would touch the candy bars in the vending machine on account of their sugar until Margaret Waller's granddaughter bought her a subscription to that there *Cosmo* magazine. Then they read that chocolate is one of those afro-dee-zee-ac foods—you know, the ones that make you frisky. And— bam—the vending guy cain't keep the machine filled fast enough. Next thing you know, they're protesting the supper menu."

That explained the last poker night. Eula had dumped an entire bag of M&M's into the Chex mix. Nikki had thought the woman had just slipped thanks to her trembling hands, but now she realized the candy had been intentional. The ladies at Golden Acres were obviously trying to sex things up.

"It's a conspiracy, I tell you," Mr. Crabtree went on. "All them bigwigs in the government think if they turn us on ourselves, females against the males, that they'll create this division. Then they can swoop right in and raise taxes and no one will be the wiser."

Mr. Crabtree hadn't paid taxes in a few decades, but Nikki didn't point that out. He was on a roll, the color in his usually pasty cheeks blazing, and she couldn't help but grin.

She dabbed a pea-size amount of gel on her hands and finger-combed it through Mr. Crabtree's thick white hair.

"Every woman wants to feel sexy once in a while. Maybe it's as simple as that."

He snorted. "The only thing we need even less than higher taxes is a bunch of oversexed eighty- and ninety-year-olds. I can barely lift the lid on the toilet, let alone anything else."

"Oh." She wiped off her hands on a small towel as he leaned toward the oval mirror she'd set up on the table. "Maybe the chocolate cake would help?"

"I ate a whole case of Snickers last month, and the only thing that went through the roof was my sugar." He shook his head. "Nah, I think it's time I just accepted the fact that I'm getting old and I ain't what I used to be." He peered into the mirror and touched a few strands of hair. "Even so, I am still a mighty fine-looking man for my age. No wonder I'm a sitting duck for that Ethel Culpepper. She's the one leading the fight. Stops by my room every night to ask me if I want to watch Letterman and drink hot chocolate. I say no, but she keeps coming back."

"I'd take it easy on her. She's only human—and you are pretty hot for eighty-six."

His chest puffed. "I'm actually eighty-nine."

"No way?"

He smoothed a few more strands of hair. "I guess it ain't really Ethel's fault."

"You do have it going on in a major way."

He beamed as he reached in his pocket and pulled out a quarter. "Much obliged, little lady." He pressed it into her palm and gave her a kiss on the cheek. "You're a sweetheart."

A warmth spread through Nikki and she couldn't help but smile.

"Don't go spending that on chocolate to torture that new fella of yours," Mr. Crabtree added.

"You know about Jake?"

"Honey, everybody's heard about Jake. You don't think we just talk about tapioca all day, do you?" He winked and hobbled off toward the iced tea and sugar-free cookies being served at the snack bar.

"I say we head for the nearest vending machine and snag a candy bar." She felt as much as heard the deep voice and she whirled smack-dab into a rock-hard chest. Strong, familiar hands came up to steady her. His husky laughter rumbled in her ears. "Easy, Trouble."

"Don't do that."

"Do what?"

"Sneak up on me like that." Her gaze collided with his and her stomach bottomed out. "How long have you been standing there?"

"Long enough to know where you get your sexual appetite. How long have you been addicted to Milky Ways?"

"I'm not *addicted* to Milky Ways. I just indulge myself once in a while. What are you doing here?"

"Looking for you." He glanced around. "What are *you* doing here?"

"Most of the residents don't drive. There's a bus, but it's used mainly for field trips. Since the people here can't come to me so easily, I just come to them."

He eyed the empty containers of hair products scattered across the table. "Looks like good business."

"Hardly. Most of them are on social security and they can't really afford to get their hair done every week."

"So you do it for free?"

She patted her pocket. "I make plenty of tips."

"Sugar, you're not making enough to buy yourself lunch."

She shrugged. "It's not about that."

He stared at her long and hard then, as if he couldn't help but wonder what it was about.

"How did you find me?" she asked, eager to change the subject.

He glanced at the table and grinned. "I followed the trail of hair products."

"Very funny." She tried to calm her suddenly pounding heart, but it was no use. He was too close and too warm, his gaze much too intense. "So what do you want?"

"This." He leaned down and claimed her mouth for a long, deep, stirring kiss.

Her lips tingled and her nipples pebbled, and just like that she was hungry for him all over again.

"You asked me to play the boyfriend, so here I am." He winked. "Ready, willing and able. So tell me, Trouble, what do boyfriends and girlfriends do around town on a Sunday night?"

She had a sudden vision of Jake's hard, tanned body splayed across her daisy print sheets. "A movie," she blurted, eager to push the vision far, far away. Sexy thoughts were fine. Understandable. But no way was she taking Jake *home*.

Temporary, she reminded herself.

"Or ice cream at the Dairy Diva," she added. "Or bingo at the community center. Or the carnival again. That's about it tonight. Tomorrow night the preliminary rodeo events will start and continue through the championship. Then there's the Fall Ball on Friday."

"What were you going to do tonight?"

"Try out some different paint colors in my kitchen." She'd picked up eight different cans, including the red and the yellow.

"I could help."

"No," she blurted. The last thing—the very last thing— she wanted was to have Jake filling up her tiny kitchen. "We really should do something in public. So people can see us."

"Let's do the movie, then." He picked up her bag and winked. "After you, sugar."

Jake followed her out to the SUV and loaded her supplies into the back. "I'll follow you to your place and we can drop off your car."

She nodded and headed for home. Her heart pounded and her blood rushed in anticipation. She remembered what her mother had said about her clothes and she contemplated changing.

This isn't a real relationship. You don't have to impress him.

She didn't, no matter how much she suddenly wanted to.

Five minutes later, she still wore her baggy jeans and T-shirt. She straddled the bike behind him and wrapped her arms around his waist. The engine roared, the bike jerked, and then they were zooming through town, headed for the small theater that sat at the corner of Main and Fourth.

Jake steered into a parking spot near the curb and Nikki climbed off. He retrieved her purse from the saddlebags draped across the bike and handed it to her.

"What do you have in that thing? Rocks?"

"Lemon drops," she blurted. "Two pounds of them."

As the realization hit, guilt rose inside of her like a tidal wave that welled and crashed, hauling her back under.

She closed her eyes and shook her head. "I don't believe it."

"What's wrong?" She heard the concern in his voice a heartbeat before she felt his fingertips brush along her cheekbone, beckoning her to look at him. "Nikki? What is it?"

"Poker night." Her gaze collided with his. "I forgot poker night. At the seniors' center." She shook her head again. "I *never* forget poker night."

Until Jake.

He'd walked in, kissed her and—bam—the only thing she'd been able to think of had been him.

"I can't believe I forgot." But it was all too believable. *Like mother, like daughter.*

"I'm sure they'll forgive you."

The thing was, Nikki wasn't so sure she could forgive herself. She'd known Jake roughly forty-eight hours, and despite her best efforts, she was letting him rearrange her priorities.

"I have to call them." She started for a nearby pay phone. "I need to apologize."

"No, you don't." Jake reached for her hand.

She tried to pull away. "I can't *not* call. They'll worry about me."

"No, they won't." She tugged her hand, but he tugged harder, hauling her a few inches before she managed to dig in her heels again.

"What makes you so sure?"

"Because you're going." His words killed her resistance as he pulled her toward the bike, his expression so fierce, so determined, so *compassionate,* that she could almost believe he wanted more from her than just a moment's pleasure. "We both are."

FOR THE FIRST TIME in over a hundred years Jake McCann was playing poker again.

Only this time, instead of beating the pants off a table of roughneck cowboys, he was losing to a blue-haired lady named Ethel.

"I'll see your piddly five," she told him, "and raise you ten." She slid the bright yellow pieces of sugarcoated candy toward the middle of the table.

"That's too rich for my blood." Nikki set her cards on the table. "I'm out. Literally." She stared at the empty spot where her own stash had once sat before shifting her gaze to the woman next to her.

"Me, too," Beula said.

The sentiment echoed around the table until the only one still in the game was Jake. But not for long. Ethel had all but wiped him out and this was his last hand if he didn't win.

He stared at the two of a kind, slid his last pieces of candy toward the middle. "Let's see what you've got."

Ethel smiled, her old face cracking into a mass of wrinkles as she fanned out a royal flush. "Read 'em and weep, children." The old woman didn't even wait to see his inferior two of a kind before she gathered up the pile of candy and pulled it toward her. "I thank you and my grandsons thank you. This is plenty to fill up my jar for their next visit."

"She cheats, I tell you," Beula said. "It just ain't natural that one woman can be that lucky."

"It ain't luck. It's skill. I told you, I use that computer my son give me for more than just looking at pictures of his little ones. I practice. And ever'body knows that practice makes perfect. Take Nikki, for instance. She had no clue what a full house was when she first started playing with us a few years back. Now she can hold her own most of the time."

Nikki winked. "What can I say? I learned from the best." She smiled at Ethel before shifting her attention to Jake. "So, are you up for another round?"

He shook his head. "I've had my butt whipped one too many times tonight. Miss Ethel," he grinned, "it's been a real pleasure. You're most certainly one of the best players I've ever seen, and I've seen my fair share."

"He's smart as well as handsome," Ethel said, winking at Nikki. "You picked a winner this time."

Nikki's gaze collided with Jake's and her thoughts echoed through his head as crystal clear as if she whispered the words directly into his ear.

If only Ethel knew that hot and hunky, here, had his hang-ups just like any other man in her past. Not that he wore women's shoes or fantasized about his mother, but he did have a thing for sex.

Then again, judging by the two chocolate shakes Ethel had consumed during their last game, the old woman might consider that more a plus than a negative.

"I'm afraid I've taken a beating, too," Nikki said, her gaze shifting back to Ethel. "I need to go lick my wounds."

"And I need to help her," Jack added.

"I'm calling it a night, too," Beula said.

The sentiment echoed around the group and Ethel shrugged. "Party poopers, all of you." She glanced at her clock. "Not that that's a bad thing. If I can hurry, I can still make some of Letterman." She winked at Nikki. "I think I'll ask Crabtree to join me."

"Don't get upset if he plays hard to get."

"Child, it's the game I live for, not the prize." Ethel winked and pushed to her feet.

Nikki gathered up her purse and Jake reached for his cowboy hat.

He tipped the brim. "Until next time, ladies."

"Wednesday night," Ethel called after them. "Same time. Same place."

"You play on Wednesday nights, too?" Jake asked as he held the door open for Nikki. She walked past him and he followed her out.

"What can I say? I've got a weakness for lemon drops."

"I think the weakness is for the ladies, not the candy." Jake kept time next to her as they headed down the front walk. The porch light pushed back the shadows a few feet and then the darkness closed around them. "They're a nice bunch of folks. I can see why you like to hang out with them."

"You're the only one." She shook her head. "Can you believe their families just abandoned them? I mean, a few of them have sons and daughters who visit, but for the most part they're alone."

He shrugged. "Being alone has its perks. Nobody telling you what to do or how to do it or when."

"Spoken like a true free spirit."

But he wasn't. He never had been. He'd always had someone or something calling the shots. First his mother, then Mr. Caskey, then the damnable hunger.

"Still," she went on, "as crazy as my mother and my aunt make me, I wouldn't trade them." A smile played at her lips. "But I would consider a temporary loan if you're interested."

"Sorry. I've had my fill of crazy relatives."

She arched an eyebrow. "Your mom?"

He nodded. Just a nod. He wasn't much for talking. He never had been. As a kid, the more he'd kept his mouth shut, the more hope he'd had of blending into the walls when his mother had been on a binge. When he'd grown older, he'd simply avoided opening his mouth because the less he'd talked about things, the easier it had been to keep his mind on work.

"She was an alcoholic," he heard himself say. "When she got loaded, she wasn't very pleasant to be around. Unfortunately she was loaded 24-7, which was why I ended up living with Mr. Caskey. He was a rancher who lived outside the town where I was born. My mother handed me over to him when I was nine, and that was the last I saw of her."

"I'm sorry. I think."

He felt a grin tug at his lips. As painful as the memories were, there was something oddly soothing about walking next to Nikki. "Being at Caskey's was a lot different than being with her. No staying up all night. No liquor. I went to

bed at the same time, got up at the same time and worked."
Caskey had been the opposite of his mother. He'd been
sober. Quiet. Emotionless. At the same time, he'd been just
as controlling. Only he'd used his fists instead of his words.

"What about school?"

"Caskey's wife taught me everything I needed to know."
Helen had taught Jake to read and write when her husband
hadn't been looking. She'd hidden books out in the bunk-
house and slipped him an extra apple in his lunch. She'd
liked him. She'd liked all kids. That's why she'd been so
desperate to have her own.

She'd died in childbirth—her and the baby—when Jake
had been sixteen. Their deaths had turned Caskey into even
more of a hard-ass, and he'd ridden Jake that much more.

"I know it was probably hard leaving your mother, but
at least you had a better life with people who wanted you."

"Caskey didn't want me." Jake wasn't sure why he told
her. He never revealed more of himself than was absolutely
necessary. He evaded questions, kept his distance, kept
moving. But suddenly he wanted her to know the truth. Part
of it, at least. "My mother stole money from him. Instead
of pressing charges, he agreed to let me work off the debt."

"But you were a child." Her touch on his hand stopped
him cold. He turned to see her eyes blazing with outrage.
"That's against the law."

"Only if someone reports it." And only nowadays. But
back then… He shrugged. "Caskey wanted his due and meant
to get it one way or another. He needed an extra pair of hands
and he didn't mind my age." In fact, he'd liked it. Jake had
been easier to intimidate. "At least I got to eat regularly."

That still doesn't make it right. The silent thought gleamed in her eyes and it was as if her soft voice whispered directly into his ear.

It did.

He could hear her thoughts. As loudly as she could hear his if he wanted her to. Because they'd had sex. They were now connected. While the link wasn't as strong as it would have been if he'd also bitten her, it was still there. Fragile but real.

She slipped her hand into his, entwining their fingers as they started to walk again.

"How long did you stay with Caskey?" she asked.

"Too long." Jake had been twenty-five by the time he'd worked off his mother's debt. A grown man. At the same time, he'd been as scared as a kid when he'd ridden past the front gate and left behind the only world he'd ever known. It was no wonder he'd hooked up with the first friendly face. And married her.

"And I thought my childhood was bad," she told him, her voice light.

"Neglect is abuse in and of itself."

"Maybe, but I had my aunt Izzie to pick up the slack. She went overboard with the attention, so that sort of cancels out the fact that my mother didn't. Izzie was always giving too much, my mom too little."

"And you were caught in the middle."

"I still am."

"You don't have to be."

"Says you. I've tried tuning them out, but it doesn't work."

"You could walk away."

"That's your thing." She tried to play off his words, but he could tell by the gleam in her eyes that she wasn't as immune to the pain as she wanted him to think. "I wouldn't want to steal your thunder."

"I thought sex was my thing."

"That, too. You're a double whammy." *Just my rotten luck.*

Jake stiffened as he heard her silent thought. *Tune her out.* That's what he told himself.

But he wouldn't do it.

He didn't want to. Just as he didn't want to be another in a long, endless string of bad luck as far as men were concerned. He wanted to be different. Because she was different.

She had a heart even bigger than her sexual appetite. She cared about people. Her mother who'd neglected her. Her aunt who smothered her. Her friends. The seniors at the retirement home. She was living out a charade with him to avoid tarnishing her aunt's image. She was spending her Sundays doing hair when she could have been at home enjoying her free time.

But that was Nikki. Selfless. Caring. *Different.*

He'd never met a woman like her, and she'd never met a man like him.

She just didn't realize it yet.

"Come on." He took her hand, his fingers twining with hers as he headed toward his motorcycle.

13

THEY DIDN'T GO TO the Skull Creek Inn, much to Nikki's surprise.

Rather, Jake zoomed past the motel and headed for her house. She braced herself for a fight as he killed the engine and followed her to the door.

Not that she feared he would try to force himself inside. He wouldn't have to. If he kissed her, touched her, stirred her the way he had the night before—and the night before that—she knew she would welcome him inside with open arms, and that's what really frightened her.

"Look—" she started, but he cut her off with the cool press of one fingertip against her lips.

"I know what you think, but I'm not like all the other men in your past. I'm different. We're different." Before she could respond, he kissed her.

It was a kiss unlike any other. His mouth feathered over hers. So soft. Sweet. Tender.

And then it was gone.

He was gone.

Her eyelids fluttered and she found herself staring at the empty spot where he'd stood only seconds before. Her gaze swiveled to the motorcycle parked at the curb in time to see him straddle the black-and-chrome monster.

He'd moved so fast. Too fast.

That or she'd been so lost in the moment that she'd been extremely slow to recover.

It was an excuse. Like so many others she'd made where he was concerned. But it eased the anxiety that niggled her and soothed the gut feeling that told her something wasn't right.

I'm different.

The engine roared in her ears as he gunned it. Kicking the bike into gear, he sent the motorcycle racing down the street, and disappointment welled deep inside.

She watched as he rounded the corner and disappeared from sight. But only when the sound had faded completely did she finally turn and go inside.

Because he might change his mind.

Because she wanted him to.

The realization followed her down the hallway and into the kitchen. She hit the light and flipped on the radio. Brooks & Dunn belted out a steady country two-step. Reaching for a screwdriver, she popped open a gallon of Aunt Izzie's Sunshine Yellow. She dipped a brush into the bright thickness and dabbed at the face of one cabinet.

She spent the next four hours going from one cabinet to the next. But no matter how much she painted, she couldn't shake the niggle of regret that ate at her. Need gnawed at her, so hungry and unrelenting, and her hands trembled. Her thighs ached and her nipples throbbed. With every stroke of the brush she imagined Jake touching her, feathering his hands over her skin.

And she thought *he* was the sex maniac?

She was a hypocrite. Here she'd been determined to prove his guilt when the entire time she'd had a great big *Do Me* stamped in the middle of her forehead.

At the same time, she didn't just find herself thinking about the way he kissed or stroked or drove her to the most exquisite orgasm. No, what she couldn't seem to push out of her mind was the quick way he'd abandoned the movie idea in favor of a night of poker with a bunch of old ladies. He'd looked so determined and compassionate as he'd steered her back toward the bike and taken off for the retirement home.

As if he'd realized how much it had meant to her.

As if he'd cared.

He didn't, and she didn't want him to. She reserved the whole caring-and-sharing thing for a real relationship, one that involved a bona fide Nice and Reliable prospect.

This…this was all about sex.

It wasn't real.

That's what Nikki told herself. She just wasn't so sure she still believed it.

FORGET BEING A VICIOUS, blood-drinking vampire.

He was a *crazy,* vicious, blood-drinking vampire.

That's what Jake realized as he stood in front of the dilapidated gas station that sat on the far edge of town.

He should be back at Nikki's place, sinking inside her warm body, soaking up all that delicious energy.

Instead he was here.

He walked around the deserted building, his gaze missing nothing despite the blanket of darkness. He saw everything from the rusted-out metal patches in the walls to a tiny spider weaving its magic on the other side of the dirty, grimy front window. He closed his fingers over the padlock on the side garage. Just the smallest amount of pressure and it crackled and snapped.

Jake unhooked the lock and pulled off the chain. He lifted the handle. Metal creaked and popped and the door rolled back. He ducked inside, his boots sliding across the dusty pavement as he surveyed the interior. It wasn't nearly as small as it looked on the outside. There was plenty of room for a fabricating table, tool stands, a few welding stations.

A doorway led into the front space where a beat-up cash register still sat on the scarred countertop. It would be tricky, but with a little careful placement he could fit a file cabinet, a tricked-out computer system and a design table into the small area.

If he was going to stay.

He wasn't. He was just thinking. Dreaming. Desperate to distract himself from the damnable need that made his groin throb.

But if he *was* going to stay, this place wouldn't be so bad for a home base. While he liked the fact that his design business required him to travel, he didn't like that he had to set up makeshift work areas when it was time for the actual build. It would be much more convenient to have one work space. No more contacting Realtors for an appropriate space or searching for local equipment dealers or

renting the various machines needed to breathe life into one
of his designs. Rather, he could go through the motions
once. Here.

Home.

The thought stirred an image of Nikki's place, with its
peeling shutters and wraparound porch and monstrous yard.

Forget it, he told himself. The last thing—the very *last*
thing—he needed was a place like Nikki's when he was so
close to his freedom.

But this… Rather than tie him down, this would actually
make things easier.

He walked back through the garage, ducked back out the
door and pulled it down after him. Hooking the chain, he
tugged one of the metal rungs apart, hooked it in the next
and tightened it back together.

He peeled off the For Sale sign taped to the front
window, folded it and stuffed it into his pocket.

Not that he was seriously going to lease this particular
space in this particular hole-in-the-wall town. He was just
curious. He needed something—anything to think about
besides Nikki. And the way she'd looked—both surprised
and disappointed—when he'd merely kissed her.

His dick throbbed and he picked up his steps. He climbed
back onto his motorcycle and headed for Town Square.

He spent the next fifteen minutes sitting in the center of
the park, near the plaque that had been dedicated to the
infamous Sam Black. The brave man who'd fought for Texas.
The vampire who'd doomed Jake to a fate worse than death.

He scanned the area, committing every tree, every
shrub, every patch of grass to memory until it lived and

breathed in his mind with vivid clarity. He wanted to be familiar with the entire park so that when the time came he wouldn't be caught off guard. He would be right here. Armed. Ready.

If he fed.

The hunger stirred in his gut, faint at the moment, but Jake had no doubt it would grow. While his sexual appetite demanded sustenance far more often than the need for blood, the latter was just as fierce. He would have to feed at least once before he faced off with Sam or he'd be as good as dead.

He thought of the carnival and the throng of people. There were tons of women, yet he didn't want any of them.

He wanted only Nikki.

Her body wrapped around him.

Her sweet blood flowing into his mouth.

But even more, he wanted her to want him. *Him.* Because he was different from every other man in her past. Because she felt more for him. Because she liked him.

As much as he liked her.

The truth haunted him as he headed back to the cave and straight into the warm, bubbling spring. He swam for several minutes and tried to clear his head and soothe the fire that gripped his body. Fat chance.

By the time he stretched out on the sleeping bag and tried to close his eyes he was still as wound up as ever. His body ached, his muscles strung tight. His cock sat up straight and stiff. He blew out a deep breath and the air whispered down the length of his body, across his bare chest, his abs, his damned cock.

Desire knifed through him, cutting him to the bone and

making him grit his teeth. He was hard to the point that it hurt. Restlessness swept through him and he barely resisted the urge to bolt to his feet and haul ass back to town. To her.

He wouldn't. He'd backed off to prove himself—and he meant to do just that. The next move was Nikki's.

That's what his head said. If only the hunger for sex that had ruled him for most of his existence didn't scream something entirely different.

JAKE SPENT THE NEXT several days doing anything—everything—but having sex with Nikki.

They watched bronc riding at the fairgrounds on Monday. Went to the movies on Tuesday. Played poker with the Greyhounds on Wednesday. And watched the parade and fireworks on Thursday.

They also talked.

Jake filled her in on the details of his design business, and Nikki told him about her dream of buying out the space next to hers and adding massage and spa treatments to her list of services. She found out that Jake could handle a horse even better than a motorcycle, and he discovered that she hated artichokes and cabbage. He liked Tim McGraw and she went nuts over Toby Keith. He could touch his nose with the tip of his tongue, and she could tie a cherry stem into a knot with hers. She loved romantic comedies and he appreciated a good Western.

By the time Friday rolled around Nikki was actually starting to think that maybe there was more to Jake than his craving for sex.

Maybe he was different after all.

She turned the idea over in her mind as she got ready for the dance that night.

As much as the notion excited her, it really didn't change anything. So what if he was a decent guy? He still had *temporary* written all over him. He was leaving on Sunday.

Thankfully.

She'd not only had a week of really incredible dates, she'd also had enough mishaps to prove that the apple hadn't fallen too far from the proverbial tree. She'd forgotten two perms and a set, and slept late three—count them—*three* times because they'd stayed up so late talking. She'd forgotten to pick up Aunt Izzie's dry cleaning. And when "Real Good Man" by Tim McGraw had came on the radio, she'd nearly buzzed off little Tommy Tanner's right ear with her hair clippers.

She was living in a fog. Excited. Exhausted. Fixated.

Just the way Jolene had been with any and every man in her past.

Unlike Jolene, however, Nikki had gone out of her way to make up for her neglect. She'd compensated her clients with free gift certificates and she'd bought Aunt Izzie a new subscription to *Reader's Digest*—much to the old woman's delight—and she'd even offered to sponsor Tommy's baseball team.

Bottom line, everyone was happy.

Including Nikki.

Wrong man, she reminded herself for the countless time. *He's all wrong and you know it.*

If only being with him wasn't starting to feel so ridiculously right.

"YOU'VE SNAGGED THE perfect man," Charlie told her as he handed her a cup of punch later that evening.

They stood in the center of the Skull Creek Community Center. A dance floor had been set up in the middle and littered with sawdust. On a portable stage off to the side, a band played a lively George Strait tune. Boots slid and cowboy hats bobbed. A large row of lights sprayed colored beams in all directions. In the far corner, fountains flowed with lemonade and tropical punch. A row of cloth-covered tables offered up everything from sausage on a stick to pigs in a blanket. There were also all sorts of desserts, including homemade pecan pie and peanut-butter fudge.

"He's not only handsome and sexy," Charlie went on, motioning toward the front entrance where Jake had gone to meet Ethel Culpepper, "he's also thoughtful."

"He is," Nikki admitted as she watched Jake take the old woman's arm and lead her toward a nearby table reserved for the residents of the retirement home. Her gaze shifted to the small cluster of wildflowers attached to her own wrist. He'd actually brought her a corsage.

"It's a dance, isn't it?" he'd said when she'd simply stared at the box as if she'd never held one before.

She hadn't.

She'd gone to the prom with Ernest Bierbottom, who'd been allergic to any and everything. Not only had he not brought her so much as a lone daisy, but he'd spent the entire time wiping at his eyes and complaining about the floral arrangements situated around the room. Then he'd complained about her dress and how the dye in it made his hands itch and he'd griped about the tablecloths and how the starch made his throat feel tight. He'd been a hypo-chrondriac, and the first of many in a long line of angst-ridden men.

Nikki lifted the corsage to her nose and inhaled. The sweet smell filled her nostrils and sent warmth spiraling through her.

"You look really great," Charlie told her. "What did you do? Call Darlene for advice?"

"For your information, I did this all by myself." She glanced down at the short, fitted yellow dress and the strappy black stilettos. She'd bought the outfit on a whim last year when she'd been in Austin for a hair show. One of the models had been wearing it and she'd looked so good.

The woman had also been ten years younger and ten pounds lighter.

When Nikki had first tried it on, she hadn't looked nearly as pretty. Even more, she'd felt awkward. Exposed.

She still felt that way.

For a good cause, she reminded herself.

While Jake had been on his best behavior, that didn't mean the sex maniac didn't lie just beneath the surface. With her cover-everything-up clothes, she'd made it easy for him to retreat and play the perfect gentleman.

No more.

It was time for the real Jake McCann to step back up to the plate and show what he was made of. Despite his claim to the contrary, he really was no different from every other man in her past.

There wasn't anything special about him. Nothing

memorable. When he walked away, she would forget him as quickly as she'd forgotten everyone else.

Nikki clung tight to the thought as she tugged at the Lycra hugging her thighs and smoothed her hem. She'd almost had him back at the house. She'd seen the hungry look in his eyes when he'd drunk in the sight of her. But then he'd handed her the corsage and she'd nearly busted into tears, and so the moment had been lost.

But the night was young.

"There you are." Darlene's voice rose over the cry of a fiddle as she came up to Nikki and Charlie. "Either you dance with me or I'm boycotting sex for the next month," she told her husband.

Charlie winked at Nikki. "Duty calls." He took Darlene's hand and steered her toward the moving mass of people.

Nikki watched as they twirled and swayed in a sensuous rhythm that made her own heartbeat kick up a notch. While she'd enjoyed spending time with Jake, she'd missed the sex. Which made her mission tonight twofold—prove Jake wrong and satisfy her own lust.

"What do you say we show them how it's done?" Jake's deep voice slid into her ear as he came up behind her. Her heart skipped its next beat and a thrill shimmied down her spine.

She smiled. "Lead the way."

JAKE TRIED TO SLOW the rush of excitement as they moved onto the dance floor and she stepped into his arms.

The fast country song slowed, fading into a sweet, hip-swaying tune that required a lot more contact than he'd anticipated. Her arms slid around his neck. Her full breasts pressed against his chest. Her pelvis cradled his crotch as she moved against him with a soft, subtle side-to-side that sent a bolt of electricity straight from his hard-on to his brain.

The closeness stirred what lived and breathed inside of him and his muscles tightened. His erection grew, straining against his jeans, begging for the woman who rubbed against him with every movement of her lush body.

Her hair tickled the underside of his jaw and her soft breaths echoed in his head. She smelled sugary-sweet, as potent and intoxicating and addictive as the fluffy cotton candy she'd been eating when he'd first met her.

He'd known tonight would be hard—that he would be hard—the moment she'd opened the door and he'd seen her decked out in her short, tight dress. She had deliciously long legs and plenty of curves, and he felt every one as he held her tight. Her warmth seeped inside him and his blood rushed faster.

He slid his hand lower, from the small of her back to the swell of her sweet, shapely ass molded by the snug dress. His other hand pushed underneath the spill of her hair to cup the back of her neck.

"It's warm out tonight," he told her, eager to say something to distract himself from the sexual awareness vibrating between them. "It should be a damned sight colder for October, don't you think?"

"I'm definitely hot." She tilted her head up and her gaze met his, and he saw the split second of need that gleamed in the honey-gold depths. She licked her lips and murmured, "You look really good tonight."

"So do you." So much for talking about the weather.

"Good enough to eat," she added. Her soft words pushed past the frantic beat of his pulse and chipped away at his determination.

She obviously wanted him. And he wanted her.

More so now than ever.

He'd had the dream again. And again. And each time the images had became sharper, more distinct.

He'd seen the whites of Nikki's eyes when the hand had slid around her neck, and he'd smelled the pungent odor of her blood as it had spilled from her throat…

Sam was close. So close now that Jake felt a constant buzz of energy. The air trembled and his nerves hummed and the hunger for sex grew more fierce with each passing moment.

He needed Nikki in the worst way.

And judging by the way she was coming on to him, she needed him just as much.

Because she'd finally admitted that he was, indeed, different from every other man in her past?

Hardly. She was grasping at straws. Desperate to keep from admitting the truth.

She pressed her body to his, teasing him, pushing him toward the edge of sanity in the frantic hope that he would turn out to be every bit the sex maniac she thought.

Kiss me.

The silent plea echoed in his head, testing his resolve. His throat tightened and his lips tingled and he was close… So damned close to backing her up against the nearest wall, pressing his body to hers and tasting her full, sweet lips.

One taste, his conscience whispered. *Then you won't want her as much.*

Big friggin' chance.

He'd already shot that theory to hell. No woman had ever tempted him back for seconds. Or thirds. He knew that no matter how many times he kissed Nikki or thrust deep inside of her, it wouldn't be enough.

He knew that long after he left Skull Creek he would remember her. She would haunt his thoughts, fuel his fantasies, set the bar for any and every other woman who came after her.

He wanted to do the same for her. He wanted her to think about him, to fantasize, to *remember.*

He stiffened, fortifying his resolve, determined to resist the lush invitation of her body. He wanted to hear the words. He needed to hear them.

Different.

But Nikki wasn't of a mind to talk. She was all about action as she slid her arms around his neck, pulled his head down and touched her lips to his.

14

"MMM...YOU DEFINITELY taste good enough to eat," Nikki murmured when she finally came up for air.

Jake's eyes blazed, a molten silver that made her face burn as he stared down at her. He wore a hungry expression, his body stiff and tight beneath her hands. He was so hard that when she moved just the slightest bit against him, he flinched.

She snaked her hands up around his neck and pressed her body that much closer. She closed her eyes and let the music take control. She swayed, rubbing her own pelvis against him, feeling definite evidence that she was turning him on and pushing him to the edge.

He held himself rigid, but at the same time, his arms wrapped around her and held her as tightly as she held him. She chanced a peek to see his determined expression, the stern set of his jaw.

Okay, so maybe, just maybe, he wasn't a sex maniac.

The thought struck just as the song ended and he turned. But then he took her hand and hauled her outside, and she knew he'd reached his limit. She followed him through the parking lot, barely keeping up with him as he wound his way around car after car in search of her SUV.

They ended up near the end of one deserted row, far

away from the blaze of lights that marked the entrance to the community center.

She stood by, breathless and anxious, while he reached into his pocket to fish for her keys. His erection stretched the crotch of his jeans, pulling the material so tight that he couldn't get his large hand deep enough.

"To hell with this," he finally muttered. He pushed her back up against the car, wedged one muscular thigh between her legs and dipped his head.

This time he took the lead and his mouth devoured hers. *Mission accomplished.*

Yet she didn't feel the expected surge of victory. The only thing she felt was desperation. To feel his body closer, his tongue deeper, his arms tighter.

Nikki's toes curled and her nerves came alive and a sizzling heat swept through her. She'd missed this so much. She'd missed him. Her hands snaked around his neck, pulling him closer. Her aching breasts pressed against the tight material of her dress.

He splayed one hand at the base of her spine, pressing her closer, while his other came up to pull her neckline down until he'd exposed one breast. The air whispered across her nipple, stirring it to life a split second before the wet heat of his mouth closed over her, catching the tip between his teeth. His tongue teased and laved for a delicious moment before he drew her in, sucking so hard that she felt the pull between her legs. She clutched at his shoulders.

He caught the hem of her dress, his fingertips sliding up the inside of her thigh. His rough touch rasped and stirred as he went higher until he touched her slick folds.

"Christ," he growled. "You're not wearing any panties."

"The dress was too tight," she gasped. "I couldn't."

"Or you didn't want to?" He stared down at her, into her. One fingertip played at her slit, trailing back and forth, driving her as crazy as she'd made him earlier.

"I…" She caught her bottom lip as he dipped a finger into her steamy heat.

"I didn't catch that, sugar," he prodded. "You left them off on purpose, didn't you? Because you've been thinking about us? About this?" He pushed his finger deeper and she gasped.

"Yes," she urged. "I—I missed you."

The admission slipped past her lips before she could stop it, and a knowing light fired his gaze even brighter.

The news seemed to send a renewed sense of urgency through him. He slid his finger another decadent inch before withdrawing. He thrust again, in and out, gliding deep and working her into a frenzy. He caught her lips for another fierce kiss.

She closed her eyes, giving herself over to the exquisite sensation. She grasped at his shoulders and moved her bottom, drawing him deeper. She was so close—

The end.

He stiffened, every muscle in his body drawing tight as his hand fell away. A growl vibrated in her ears.

"Jake?" Nikki's eyes popped open—and that's when she saw him.

His eyes blazed a furious red. His sensuous mouth parted and his lips drew back, revealing a very lethal-looking pair of fangs.

She blinked.

Fangs?

They were still there. Still gleaming in the moonlight.

Impossible.

Shock jolted her, followed by a wave of panic that crashed over her, tugged her under and refused to let her come up for air.

No way.

No friggin' *way.*

He whirled then, and that's when she saw the man that stood a few feet away from them.

He was just as tall and as handsome as Jake.

And his fangs looked every bit as lethal.

"No!"

The sound of her own voice roared in her ears, drowning out the thunder of her heart. The ground seemed to shake. Her face blazed and her knees buckled.

And then everything went blessedly black.

JAKE CAUGHT NIKKI before she crumpled at his feet. He swept her legs out from under her and hiked her into his arms. Turning, he came face-to-face with the vampire who'd come up behind him.

It seemed Garret Sawyer had saved him from the hunger not once but twice now.

Only this time Jake wasn't half as thankful as he'd been that first time. He'd been desperate for blood back then, while this time had been purely sex.

Purely Nikki.

He cradled her in his arms and eyed his business partner. "You're a long way from Houston."

Garret held up his hands. "Relax, man. I didn't mean to scare you." He crossed the short distance to Jake. His eyes, which had fired to life out of pure instinct when Jake had whirled on him, had cooled to an icy blue. He wore faded jeans, an Orange County Choppers T-shirt and worn biker boots. A red-white-and-blue bandanna covered his cropped brown hair. A tiny silver skull dangled from one ear. "I thought you could use some help."

"I thought this was just another wild-goose chase to you?"

The older vampire shrugged. "It is. But if it all pans out, then you'll need my help. Sam's not going down without a fight." When Jake didn't say anything, Garret added, "Look, I'm sorry I tried to discourage you, man, I've been searching for my own maker for so long that I'm just burned out." He shrugged. "Being a vampire has its perks." He winked. "You can fly like a superhero. Lift cars like the Incredible Hulk. Wow all the ladies like Brad Pitt. It's a charmed afterlife if you think about it."

"We don't rule the power, man. It rules us."

Garret shrugged. "There are worse things." His gaze shifted to Nikki and a somber expression slid over his face. "You're feeding. He must be close."

Jake nodded. "I can feel him."

"That explains why you freaked just now. I thought you were going to rip out my throat."

"When I felt you behind me, I thought you were him."

"No such luck, my friend." He spared another glance at Nikki. "She's not your usual style, but I can certainly see the attraction. I can feel the energy coming off her."

Jake's hold on her tightened.

Garret grinned. "Don't worry, bro. You need her more than I do at this point. Besides—" he glanced toward the community center "—I saw a redhead a few minutes ago that had that come-and-get-me-baby look in her eyes." He clapped Jake on the shoulder. "I'll catch up with you later." In a flash, he reached the door to the community center and disappeared inside.

Jake nodded and turned his attention to the woman in his arms. Soft, shallow breaths sawed past her lips. Her chest rose and fell in a steady rhythm.

Gone was the panic. And the fear.

For now.

Christ, she'd *seen* him.

Dread and denial whirled together to make his gut ache and his hands tremble. Sure, she'd glimpsed the truth a time or two when his control had slipped, but it had been so quick that she'd written it off as her imagination.

But this time she'd gotten a good, long look. There were no excuses this time. No escaping the truth.

Unless…

He could make her forget. He could make anyone forget. It was a trick of the trade and one he'd used before whenever anyone got too close and saw too much. All he had to do was look into her eyes and will away the memory and everything would be cool. Nikki could go on about her business and he could go on about his.

Instinct urged him to do just that. It was the way he'd survived for so many years.

But he wanted more than survival now. He wanted his freedom.

All the more reason to kill the memory.

That's what his head said. There was no reason for her to know the truth about him. He would be in and out of her life so fast.

At the same time, he'd vowed to set himself apart, to secure a place in her memory, to prove beyond a doubt that he was different from every other loser in her past.

Men who'd held back, kept secrets, deceived her.

This was his chance to set himself apart.

The decision certainly had nothing to do with the fact that he'd been alone and lonely far too long and he'd finally reached his limit. He was tired of running. Pretending. He wanted something real. Solid. Lasting. And that meant coming clean.

Like hell.

This was all about following through. He'd wanted to set himself apart, and suddenly he couldn't think of a better way to do just that.

SHE'D SMELLED ONE TOO many containers of perm solution.

That's what Nikki told herself when her eyelids finally fluttered open and reality sank in.

She lay on her back on a soft down sleeping bag. A small lantern burned nearby, pushing back the shadows just enough for her to see that she was in a huge cave. A waterfall trickled nearby, splattering into a spring that bubbled and steamed several feet away.

"I'm glad you're awake."

Jake's voice brought her upright and she twisted to find him sitting a few feet away, his back against the cave wall.

He wore the same black jeans and white dress shirt he'd worn to the dance. The crisp shirt now hung loose, the buttons undone, the edges parted to reveal the hard, muscular chest beneath.

He looked like any other handsome, sexy man…who just happened to be sitting in the middle of a cave. His gaze deepened, shifting from molten silver to a bright purple as he regarded her.

She blinked as the past rushed at her. In her mind's eye she saw him poised above her their first night at the motel. His eyes gleamed as bright, as colorful as they were right now. He arched his neck, his lips pulled back, his fangs—

She shook away the image, but another rushed in to take its place.

The scene from the motorcycle, when Jake's hands had been on her rather than the handlebars. The bike had held steady, eating up ground so swift and straight, as if something far more powerful had been in control—

"Where am I?" she blurted, eager to kill the memory. Her gaze darted around, drinking in the jagged walls, the earth floor.

"It's a cave cut into the hills just outside of town. It's not easy to get to—but then, I needed someplace isolated to spend my days."

"You work during the day," she said as if by voicing the words out loud she could make them true. "You design motorcycles."

"I sleep during the day—I have to—and I work on my designs in the early evening." He motioned to the laptop sitting a few feet away. "And then I see you." He stared at her for a long moment. His gaze burned such a bright shade of purple that suddenly it hurt her eyes and she blinked.

As if he knew his effect on her, he glanced away. His attention shifted to their surroundings. "There isn't a trace of sunlight during the day. It's dark here. Safe. I'm at my most vulnerable during the day. I'm pretty much invincible except when it comes to wooden stakes and sunlight. The sunlight won't kill me. It just hurts like hell. But a stake through the heart…that'll turn me to dust faster than you can blink."

Because he was a *vampire*.

The notion rushed at her, fueled by the thoughts that darted in and out of her head. The eyes. The overwhelming sexiness. The way he looked so deeply at her, *into* her. As if he could see all of her secrets while she could see none of his. The fangs.

No! her conscience screamed. It couldn't be. *He* couldn't be.

"Where's my SUV?" She grasped at the first sane thought that popped into her head.

"Back at the community center."

"Then how did we get here?"

"My motorcycle."

"But that was parked back at my place. If you left the SUV at the community center, then how did we get back to my place?"

"We flew."

She was *not* hearing this.

"I don't turn into a bat," he went on. "But I can levitate and move around. I wanted to get you out of there fast and so I picked you up and carried you home."

"Why didn't you leave me there? Why…?" She shook her head. "Why am I here?"

"I wasn't about to dump you on your doorstep, and you've never invited me in. So I loaded you onto my bike, climbed on behind you and brought you here."

"But I was unconscious."

"I held you with both arms. I didn't need them for my chopper. I can control that with my mind."

Because he was a vampire rather than a man.

Crazy.

Vampires didn't exist. They were the stuff of movies and hit television shows. A myth. *A nightmare.*

And this?

Her fingers curled into the down comforter, feeling its soft warmth. Her shoes sat on the ground just to her left and she reached out. She touched the black leather, felt the smoothness against her fingertips before she let her hand fall away. She clawed at the dirt floor, felt it push beneath her fingernails. *Real.*

Her gaze shifted to Jake. He turned his head and stared at a second lantern sitting lifeless near the foot of her sleeping bag. His eyes brightened and just like that a flame flickered and burned.

The air lodged in her chest as shock beat at her already shocked brain. She bolted to her feet and rushed toward the underground spring. Dropping to her knees, she splashed the liquid onto her face. Water drip-dropped, falling onto the front of her dress, soaking through the material. She cupped her hands and leaned over, splashing more water, as if she could wash away the images that rolled through her head.

"I know this is a lot to take in." At the sound of Jake's deep, husky voice she opened her eyes. The water served as a mirror and she saw him towering behind her.

"Y-you have a reflection." She touched the water and his image rippled.

"Some of the myths are true and some aren't. I don't have any particular aversion to garlic or crosses. Holy water isn't particularly painful. And I can see myself in a mirror just like anyone else."

But he wasn't like anyone else. He was a creature of the dark. A night-stalking, blood-drinking *vampire*.

Her hand went to her throat, her fingers trailing over the smooth skin, searching.

"You didn't drink from me," she blurted.

"Yes, I did."

"But—"

"Vampires don't just feed off of blood. We also crave energy. Sexual energy."

What?

Even as the question pounded through her head, her brain scrambled for answers, fitting the pieces together as if she were racing against the clock.

Feed.

Sex.

One-night stand.

That's why he'd been at the carnival. He'd needed a woman. And so he'd picked her. "Why?" The question fell from her lips. "You could have had any woman at that carnival, but you picked me. Why?"

"You have a lusty appetite. You'd denied yourself for so

long that you were like a volcano ready to explode. I couldn't resist."

"In other words, you picked me because I was desperate."

"And you picked me because I was desperate," he reminded her. "You came to my hotel room of your own free will."

Because she'd thought that he was a regular guy. A temporary guy.

"I am temporary," he said as if reading her thoughts.

As if?

He *was* reading them.

"Just as you can read mine," he told her. "We're connected. Bound by the sex."

She shook her head. "I can't read your thoughts."

"You have to focus. Project."

Her mind raced too fast. Denial and relief and a multitude of other emotions swirled together, overloading her mental circuits.

"The telepathy is part of what I am," he went on. "When I look into someone's eyes, I can see what they're thinking. Right now you're not half as afraid of me as you are of yourself. You're afraid of the way I make you feel. Because even though you know the truth now, you're still attracted to me."

Because he was a vampire.

Forget chemistry. What flowed between them was pure lust. It oozed from Jake, courtesy of his vampness, and Nikki couldn't help but be caught up in it.

Any woman would have been.

"But I don't want any woman." His gaze caught and

held hers in the mirrorlike pool. "I want you. And you still want me."

She wanted to deny it, but what was the point?

The truth stood staring back at her, a shimmering reflection of a man who was more than a man. His eyes gleamed hot and potent and powerful. He touched her, his fingertips burning into her arm, and lust stirred, fierce and quick and far more powerful than the throb of fear keeping time with her frantic heartbeat.

His scent—raw and male and a touch savage—filled her nostrils and created the most damning thoughts of two bodies tangled together, touching and twisting and kissing. Sex at its most primitive level. Passionate. Breath-stealing. *Desperate.*

She inhaled and immediately regretted it. The scent grew stronger, the impressions more vivid. Her body trembled, urging her to turn and reach out. To touch him.

Are you crazy? her last bit of sanity demanded. *Sure, he's hot and the sex is great, but he drinks blood. One minute you're having an orgasm and the next you're on life support.*

"I never mix the blood with the sex. Drinking from someone either way forges an intense mental connection. To do both simultaneously would make that connection twice as strong. Unbreakable."

Permanent rather than temporary. And vampire or not, Jake was clearly number two.

Disappointment rushed through her, followed by a wave of indignation and a mental ass-kicking. *Are you kidding me? It's not like you ever, for even five seconds, wanted a real relationship with him.*

Okay, maybe for five seconds.

But everything had done a complete one-eighty. Jake wasn't the man she'd thought him to be. Cripes, he wasn't a man at all. He was a vampire.

Who wanted only sex from her.

She could see the truth in the hot brightness of his gaze, feel it in the heat coming from his fingertips and hear it in the raw huskiness of his voice.

"Come." It was one word, yet she was powerless to resist.

That's what she told herself.

It had nothing, absolutely *nothing* to do with the fact that she was tired of thinking. Of trying to process the truth. To believe the unbelievable. And suddenly she wanted only to feel.

She turned toward him.

15

DIFFERENT.

The word vibrated in Jake's head and kept him from pressing her up against the nearest hard surface and plunging fast and sure inside of her hot, tight body.

Instead he moved away. So fast that he knew to her it appeared as if he'd just vanished. One minute he was helping her to her feet and the next she stood at the water's edge all by herself.

"Nikki."

She whirled at the sound of her name. Her gaze zigzagged through the semidarkness until it found him on the opposite side of the underground spring.

His eyes locked with hers as he lifted his hand and trailed his fingers in midair.

When she felt the delicate touch along her cheekbones, shock jolted through her, widening her eyes and parting her full lips. Desire followed, easing her taut expression and chasing away the furrows in her forehead. Her lids grew heavy and her chest hitched.

Jake moved his attention lower, around the slope of her jaw, down the sensitive column of her neck.

Goose bumps chased down the lengths of her arms, and

her nipples pebbled, pushing tight against the bright yellow material of her dress. He licked his lips and she gasped. He knew she felt the contact even though he stood several feet away.

There was no mistaking the freight train of different emotions that barreled through her—denial, pleasure, disbelief, wonder, excitement. She felt them all.

She felt *him.*

In a way she'd never felt another man before.

Satisfaction rushed through him, followed by a surge of desire so intense that he shook from the force of it.

"I need to see you," he said, his voice gruff, his throat suddenly tight.

Nikki stared across the smooth, shimmering water to where Jake stood near the small waterfall. She watched the purposeful movement of his hand and felt the edge of her hem catch. The material slid up her thighs, over her hips, to her waist. Air whispered over her bare skin, between her legs, to tease her clitoris. Her body throbbed in response and her knees turned to jelly.

His hands moved higher and so did the dress. It caught on her breasts, snagging for a long, breathless moment before slithering up and over.

"Lift your arms." His voice was ragged this time, betraying his calm, controlled demeanor.

She had the distinct impression that while he was the vampire who called the shots, she was the one in control.

She wasn't, she reminded herself. Despite the fierce longing that flashed in his gaze. The desperation.

I want you.

His voice murmured through her head so loud and clear, and she knew then that he spoke the truth. They were telepathically linked now. He'd invaded her body and her mind.

And her heart.

Nikki fought the truth and clung to the lust burning her up from the inside out. Her heart had nothing to do with any of this. It was all about her body. She slid her palms into the air.

The dress slithered up and over her head and fell into a yellow puddle beside her. A thread of heat snaked around her ankles and worked its way up as she stood there naked and breathless. The sound of trickling water filled her ears, mingling with the frantic beat of her heart.

He studied her for an endless moment and his eyes fired an even brighter, more intense shade of purple.

Desire. His deep, husky voice whispered through her head even though his lips never moved. *My eyes are this color when I'm turned on.*

The breath caught in her chest and her head started to spin again. Her nipples grew tighter, harder, eager to be stroked, nibbled, sucked. *Now.* Anticipation coiled in the pit of her stomach and her legs trembled.

He stepped toward her, his boots skimming the top of the water as he crossed the pool.

"What about you, Nikki? Are you turned on?" He came to a stop right in front of her, so close she could almost touch him.

If she reached out.

"I…" She licked her suddenly dry lips. "What do you think?"

"I think," he murmured, his thumb grazing the very tip of her breast, "that you're about as worked up, as *wet* as a woman can get." The words slid into her ears to stroke across her nerve endings. "You've never been this hot for any other man, have you?" She shook her head and satisfaction brightened his eyes. "Show me. Show me how much you want me."

Me and only me.

She could no more deny him than she could fly to the moon and back. The lust burned too fierce, blazing inside of her, fueling her with an urgency to touch him. Taste him. Regardless of what he was.

Because of it.

She knew that was the cause for her sudden desperation and she grasped at the explanation rather than consider the alternative—that she reached out not because he was more than any other man she'd ever been with but because he was *the* man.

She focused on the desire raging inside her and grasped the edges of his shirt. Flesh grazed flesh as she pushed the material over his shoulders, down his arms, until it fell away and joined her discarded dress. She reached for the waistband of his jeans.

A groan rumbled from his throat as her fingertips trailed over the denim-covered bulge. She worked the zipper down, tugging and pulling until the teeth finally parted. The jeans sagged on his hips, and his erection sprang hot and greedy into her hands.

She traced the ripe purple head before sliding her hand down his length, stroking, exploring. His dark flesh throbbed against her palm and her own body shuddered in response. She licked her lips, suddenly eager to taste him. A crazy reaction for a woman who'd never been all that fond of giving a blow job.

But this was Jake. Every reaction she'd ever had with him had been off the charts because of the lust she felt for him.

The lust he inspired.

She dropped to her knees, smoothed her fingers down the dark perfection of his shaft and took him into her mouth. She laved and suckled for a long moment before he grasped her shoulders and stilled her movements.

"Don't," he groaned.

She pulled away and glanced up to find him staring down at her.

"I…" he started, but words seemed to fail him. Surprise flashed in his gaze, followed by a fleeting uncertainty. Where he'd wanted to set himself apart from the men in her past, she had the distinct feeling that she'd just set herself apart from the women in his.

"It's not about my pleasure," he told her. "It's about pleasuring you. That's when I gain the most energy. I drink it in when you climax." He shook his head. "I do the pleasuring, not the other way around."

Until now.

Until Nikki.

Because she wasn't his usual woman and this wasn't his typical liaison. It was more.

She was more.

Hope flared inside of her, only to die a quick death as she snuffed it out and focused on the fierce, sexy picture he made towering over her.

He was massive, his chest broad and muscular. His arms hung at his sides, the familiar tattoos encircling both biceps. His face was flushed, his eyes bright and glittering.

"You're so beautiful," he said, his voice laced with awe as he traced a fingertip along her cheekbone, the curve of her jaw, her chin. "So beautiful and so damned perfect."

A rush of warmth went through her, a reaction that had nothing to do with the lust beating at her senses and everything to do with the reverent way he touched her, as if he couldn't quite believe she was real.

She knew the feeling.

A *vampire*.

Her mind still reeled from what she'd seen and felt. But there was no denying that it was real. Not when she could feel the warm muscles of his thighs beneath her palm and taste the salty sweetness of him on her lips.

She trailed her tongue over her bottom lip and he groaned.

Hands reached for her and she found herself pulled into the solid comfort of his arms. He kissed her, plunging his tongue inside to explore and savor until she gasped for breath. She felt his erection, hard and eager against her stomach, promising the ecstasy to come, making her painfully aware of the throbbing and the wetness between her own legs.

When he moved his mouth to nibble a path down her neck, she tilted back her head. Pleasure rushed to her brain and the anticipation built. He licked his way down the slope of her breast.

He found her nipple and she gasped. She buried her hands in his hair, holding him close, arching her breast into the moist heat of his mouth.

But it wasn't enough. She needed to get closer. Faster.

He read her desperation, locked her in his powerful arms and lifted her. The head of his penis nudged between her legs and the word ▮▮▮▮▮ popped into her head.

"Wait—" she gasped, but he silenced her with a quick, desperate kiss.

"You won't catch anything from me," he murmured against her lips. While it was probably the oldest line when it came to sex, she knew it was a valid one in this particular situation.

Because Jake wasn't the typical sexually active male. He was much, much more.

For now.

His voice whispered through her head and she opened her mouth to question him. But then he urged her down in one swift thrust, and whatever she'd been about to say faded into a groan. Pleasure burst through her and the air lodged in her chest.

She clung to him, wrapping her legs around him as he buried himself deep. The delicious fullness sent jolts of electricity chasing up and down the length of her spine.

She didn't know when he moved them. But one minute they were standing on the side of the underground spring and the next they were sinking slowly into the warm water.

The liquid welcomed them, gliding up over their skin until they were up to their waists.

Grasping at his shoulders, she held on tight as he cupped her buttocks and urged her to move. The water lapped at her bottom, sloshing and stirring, feeding the sense of urgency that grew each time she slid up, then down. Grasp and release. Over and over. Again and again.

When she felt the first wave of pleasure, she dug her nails into his flesh and held on as sensation rocked her body. Her head fell back and she clamped her eyes shut as heat drenched her and stole the oxygen from her lungs.

His groan slid past the thunder of her own heart, and she forced her eyes open in time to see him. His eyes blazed back at her. Hot. Bright. Like twin violet laser beams. The tendons in his neck tightened. His jaw clenched. His mouth fell open and his fangs gleamed in the dim light.

Fangs! her sanity screamed.

She had the fleeting thought that she should be terrified at that particular moment. But the pleasure was too intense, her orgasm too overwhelming. She tightened her body around him, milking him as he moaned, long and low and deep. He came then in a rush of bubbling wetness, his body bucking, his muscles strung tight.

He hauled her close and buried her head against his neck for several long, breathless moments. Nikki clung to him, relishing the feel of his pulse beat against her lips.

So steady and sure and *real*.

As real as the vampire who held her.

The truth sank in as they stood there in the water and held each other, his heart beating solidly against her own.

He really *was* a vampire.

Why…? How…? When…? Where…?

The questions rushed at her, so many that she didn't know which one to ask first. Jake saved her the trouble of having to decide.

"I was turned back in 1883," he murmured as he pulled away and stared down at her. "Not too far from here, in a small town called Junction."

"I know that town."

He nodded. "It's a lot bigger now than it was back then." He gathered her close and waded from the water. The liquid drip-dropped, the sound following them as he carried her over to the sleeping bag and eased her down. "I was thirty at the time."

He sat down next to her and pulled his legs up. He braced his elbows on top of his knees and stared straight ahead. The tight line of his mouth told her that he didn't see the cave wall at all. Rather, he saw his past as the words started to flow. "Contrary to popular myth, you don't turn into a vampire just by being bitten by one. You must drink the blood of a vampire." He clasped his hands, his knuckles tight. "I was attacked by one who then forced me to drink his blood."

She wanted to say something, but she was too busy absorbing his words to form any of her own.

"I didn't want to," he went on, his voice low, almost hesitant, "but he'd all but ripped out my throat and I didn't have a choice. I tried to fight, but it was no use." He shrugged. His powerful shoulders shook and her chest tightened.

"That must have been terrible." The words were out before she could stop them. Not that she would have. While the situation itself still seemed so unreal, his pain was all too real.

"The really terrible part came later. When I woke up, there was no sign that I'd ever been attacked. My throat was in one piece. There was no blood. Not even a scar. Nothing but this strange tingling in my gut that told me something was different." He shook his head. "At first I could still walk in the sunlight. But with each day that passed it started to bother me more and more, until it became painful. And then I had these urges..." He shook his head. "I didn't act on them. I fought the hunger, but eventually it got the best of me."

Silence settled between them as Nikki absorbed the story while he relived it in his head. The loneliness. The desolation. The horror.

His voice was quiet when he finally spoke. Pained. "I almost killed a man. I was so crazed with thirst that I attacked him. I would have killed him in a hungry rage if not for Garret."

"Garret? Your partner?"

He nodded. "I'd never met him before that moment. He's the one who found me just as I was about to rip this cowboy's face off. Garret stopped me and let me drink from his own vein until the hunger calmed enough for me to come to my senses. Before then I had no idea what I was. My wife had just run off and our place was going to hell in a handbasket. I felt so sick that I couldn't work the horses. I thought I was dying, but then I met Garret and found out that I'd already died."

"So she really did leave you."

"I told you the truth. Just not all of it." He scrubbed a hand over his face. "I wouldn't have made it without Garret. He was turned back during the Texas Revolution, a good fifty years before me."

"That's right around the time that Skull Creek was founded."

He nodded. "He was older, wiser. He'd already figured out how to control the hunger for blood. The trick is to feed it slowly, regularly. Also, the older a vampire is, the longer he can go before he has to quench his thirst. He taught me that, as well."

"It was him, wasn't it? At the community center?"

He nodded. "Vampires can sense other vampires. I sensed Garret's presence before I realized it was him and, of course, I shifted into survival mode." His gaze caught and held hers. "I wasn't going to let anyone hurt you, Nikki."

A protective light gleamed in his eyes, and she felt a rush of warmth from her head to the tips of her toes.

"What about the hunger for sex?" she asked, suddenly eager to ignore the strange feeling. The lust, she could handle. But this... "Do you have to feed it often?"

He nodded. "Ideally once a day. Sometimes more. The less blood I drink, the more sex I need. I'm a slave to both." He shrugged. "But then, that's the story of my life."

She remembered the story about his childhood and suddenly it made sense. He hadn't slipped between the cracks. He'd been born and raised in a time where there'd been no services to protect children and so he'd been caught in a bad situation. *Enslaved.*

She reached out, her fingers trailing over the tattoo that encircled his left bicep.

"Is that why you got the tattoos?"

"I'm a vampire, sugar. We're invincible to most every-thing, including needles." He shook his head. "I didn't do this to myself. It came with the territory. A reminder that while I have a shitload of power compared to the average Joe Blow, it comes from a higher source. One that calls the shots in everything I do." He laughed, a hollow, heart-breaking sound. "I always thought that once I worked off my mother's debt to Caskey I would be free, but that didn't happen. I rode straight from his place to the nearest town and hooked up with the first woman who smiled at me. And just like that, I found myself caught in another bad situation. Then I was attacked and it went from bad to worse. One prison to the next. Stuck."

She knew the feeling. She'd been stuck between her mother and her aunt her entire life. Making someone else's choices, living someone else's dream.

She was still doing it.

Sure, she'd bought her own house, but she had several gallons of yellow and red sitting in her kitchen despite the fact that she wasn't one hundred percent crazy about either of them. She liked them both.

Stuck.

"Pick the color that you like," he told her, his gaze drilling into hers, reading her thoughts. "You don't have to be what they want you to be. You can be yourself."

But could she?

"So what happened next?" she blurted, eager to change the sudden direction of the conversation. "After you met Garret and realized this was a permanent thing?"

"I accepted my fate. I had to. I moved from town to town, living for a little while, blending, until it was time to move on. I worked horses mostly. Tended herds. Times changed, but the need for good cowboys didn't. I kept working horses over the years, moving from ranch to ranch, place to place."

"When did you get interested in motorcycles?"

"I started riding back in the sixties. That's when I started to fiddle with machinery and my interests switched from horseflesh to steel. The motorcycles lend themselves to the same type of wandering lifestyle. My destiny—or so I thought. But then I met this man about ten years ago. He was an old man. Crazy Cooter. That's what people called him. He told me this story about how he'd once been a vampire but he'd escaped the hunger by killing the vampire who'd turned him." Another shake of his head. "It was wild, but it turns out he was telling the truth. I looked into his eyes and I knew, and that's when I realized I didn't have to keep living like this. If I could find my sire, I could break free."

"So what have you been doing in the ten years since?"

"Looking. I didn't have much to go on. Just a name. But it was enough. I've tracked down every Sam Black from here to—"

"Wait a second," she cut in. "*Sam Black? The* Sam Black who founded this town? *He's* the one who turned you? But he's a hero."

"He stopped being a hero the day he was attacked and killed by those Mexican bandits."

Her mind started to race. "You mean…?"

"They were vampires. They didn't just kill him. They turned him. That's why no one found a body. He was turned smack dab in the middle of town—and he'll go back there Sunday."

"Why?"

"It's the turning instinct. We all have it. Every year, on the exact date that a vampire is turned, at the exact moment, he must return to the spot where death ended and life began again. The afterlife. He feels the pain again and relives the moment where his soul fled and the hunger took its place."

"That sounds awful."

"It feels a hundred times worse. But it's a must. We all do it. I prepare for it by making sure that I have a blood source on hand to feed so that I don't hurt anyone during those few seconds when I lose control."

"A blood source? Like what?"

"A dead animal or even a few bags of the bottled stuff from a local blood bank. It's hard to come by but possible. Garret dated a woman who worked at one last year, so I had plenty when my time came. But I doubt Sam takes the same precautions." His gaze met hers. "There are vampires out there who relish the change. They like the wildness."

"You think Sam is like that? But he's—was—a hero."

"The hunger has a way of changing you. It can bring out the worst if you let it." His mouth drew into a determined line. "Sam won't get the chance to doom anyone else. This year I'll be waiting for him. I'll destroy him while he's mindless and in the middle of reliving the experience, and by destroying the source I'll be free of the hunger. In less than forty-eight hours," he went on, "I'll be human again."

The realization of his words struck and hope fired to life inside her.

"I'll be able to walk in the sunlight and eat real food

and live a normal life. I'll walk away from here really and truly free."

Regret welled, snuffing out the hope as quickly as it had flared.

"For the first time in my life," he went on, "I won't have anyone or anything dictating my actions. Do you know what that means?"

That while he'd turned out to be a vampire rather than a man, he was still every bit as temporary as she'd originally thought.

And the problem was?

No problem, she told herself. It wasn't as if she wanted a happily ever after with him. Far from it. Sure, he was hot and hunky and he'd given her the best sex of her life, but only because he was a vampire.

Jake the man wouldn't have the same effect on her.

Even as she told herself that, she knew it was a lie. Because she'd seen more than just a vampire this past week. She'd seen the man, too. And damned if she didn't like him just as much.

Love him, even.

The notion stirred a wave of panic and sent her scrambling to her feet. She didn't love him, but it would be easy to fall in love with him if she didn't end things right here and now.

"What's wrong?" his voice followed her, his gaze drinking in her frantic movements as she hurried to retrieve her dress.

"I really need some air." Air that didn't smell like Jake. Or feel like Jake. She jerked on the yellow material and pushed it down over her hips. "It's getting really late. I should go home." She snatched up her shoes and started for the only visible exit, a monstrous hole that gaped dark and ominous, ready to swallow her up.

"Nikki, wait!"

But she couldn't.

She had to get away from him before she did something really stupid like throw herself into his arms and beg him to stay.

"Nikki!" Her name rang out a second before he caught her arm in a firm jerk that brought her whirling around to face him. "What's wrong with you?"

"Me? There's nothing wrong with me. It's you. *You,*" she blurted. "You're no different than the rest of them. They all had their own hidden agenda and so do you."

"What are you talking about?"

"You're leaving here."

You're leaving me.

The thought hung in the air between them as she stared up at him and he stared down at her, into her.

"Stay with me tonight." His voice was low, husky, compelling. "Please."

She wanted to. She wanted to so much that it scared her and made her fight that much harder. Because she'd never wanted a man the way she wanted Jake McCann.

She shook her head frantically and pushed at his hands. "I can't. I won't."

She might want him, but she didn't *need* him. Nor did she love him. Sure, she was falling. Stupidly, blindly falling, but she intended to catch herself. Now. Before it was too late.

She yanked free and stumbled blindly forward, feeling

her way down the dark, winding cave until she broke free into a small clearing. Moonlight pushed down through the trees, lighting up the darkness.

She was about to pick a direction when she heard the grumble of his motorcycle. A few frantic heartbeats later, he pulled up beside her.

"Get on."

"I'll walk."

"You don't know where the hell you are."

She was scared not stupid, so she climbed onto the back of his bike, slid her arms around him for the last time and held on while Jake sent the bike roaring through the trees.

When he pulled up in front of her house a good half hour later, it took everything she had to pull away from him and walk up the sidewalk. Her hands trembled as she unlocked her door and walked inside the house. She chanced a glance behind her, to where the black-and-chrome motorcycle idled by the curb. Jake stared back at her, his hands tight on the handlebars, his body taut, as if it took all of his strength not to go after her and force his way in.

He couldn't. He had to be invited. He'd said so himself. But even if he would have been able to, she knew deep in her heart that he wouldn't. Because as much as she wanted him to stay, he wanted to go.

He had to.

She closed the door and headed upstairs. Nikki peeled off her dress, pulled on her favorite sweats and climbed into bed.

And then she cried.

16

JAKE HIT THE interstate and opened up the throttle. The engine roared, the wheels eating up asphalt at a frenzied pace. It was close to four in the morning and he had only a few hours until daylight. Not that he cared. His thoughts were still back at Nikki's place.

What the hell did she expect from him?

He had to leave. This was his chance. His one shot to really and truly live for himself rather than someone—or something—else.

He was taking it. He wanted to take it.

The wind slapped at his face. The rubber handlebars dug into his palms. The bike vibrated with a fury that seeped into him and made him clench his teeth. He could feel the sharpness of his fangs cutting into his tongue and he tasted the sticky sweetness of his blood.

His gut churned. His pulse raced.

He'd been holding out for so long. Too long.

He needed to feed.

For the first time Jake held tight to the craving that welled deep inside him. Heat fired to life, spreading through him like wildfire during a Texas dry spell. He burned from the inside out, and there was only one thing that could quench the flames.

Blood.

His gaze snagged on a neon sign that flashed in the distance and he took the next exit. Slamming on his brakes, he cut to the right and pulled into a 24-hour truck stop. It wasn't much to look at, just a faded building with grimy windows and a dirt parking lot.

Everything from eighteen-wheelers to four-door pickups filled the massive lot. Inside, lights blazed and bodies filled every table and booth. The smell of bacon and eggs wafted from the double doors as a group of men walked outside.

Jake found a parking spot, killed the engine and climbed from his bike. A bell tingled as he pushed open the door and walked inside. He stood there for several long seconds, surveying the interior, from the jukebox and cigarette machine to a pie display just off to his left. His gaze flitted this way and that until he spotted a woman sitting at the counter. Her hair wasn't as blond as Nikki's and she had dull brown eyes rather than vibrant gold. She wore a tank top, worn jeans and a used expression that said she was fed up with everyone and everything.

He picked his way through the maze of tables and slid onto the stool next to her.

"Welcome to CeCe's," a waitress told him as she set a piece of laminated plastic on the counter in front of him. "Just have a look-see at the menu. Then give a holler and let me know what you want."

Jake turned, his gaze colliding with dull brown eyes.

He didn't need a look-see. He knew what he wanted, and it was sitting right beside him.

"You look like shit," Garret told him when Jake rolled into the cave barely an hour before sunup. The vampire sat stretched out on a plaid bedroll, his back to the wall, a laptop balanced on his knees. "What happened?"

Jake climbed off his bike and walked over to the underground spring. Kneeling, he cupped his hands and splashed water onto his face. "I got into a fight," he said once he came up for air. Water drip-dropped from his bruised and swollen face and splattered the front of his soiled shirt.

"Excuse me?" Garret stared at him as if he'd grown two heads. But then, he probably looked just as strange. His left eye was almost swollen shut. A cut oozed on his forehead.

He noted the sudden brightness in Garret's eyes when the vampire caught sight of the wound, and Jake knew that while his friend had fed tonight, he'd done it with sex rather than blood.

"What the hell happened?" Garret pressed.

"I got my ass kicked by a guy named Bubba."

"How does a vampire get his ass kicked by anybody?"

"I don't want to talk about it."

"I guess not." Garret shook his head, his earring catching the glare from his computer screen. "I'd be embarrassed, too."

But Jake wasn't embarrassed. He was relieved.

Miss Brown Eyes had turned out to be a hooker. While she'd been more than willing to let him do any and everything—including sinking his fangs into her—her pimp of a boyfriend hadn't had the same idea. He'd followed them outside and confronted Jake before he could even touch the woman. He'd pulled out a baseball bat and demanded payment up front.

Jake had realized then that he hadn't even bothered to read the woman's thoughts. He'd been so wrapped up in his own feelings, so angry and hurt and desperate, that he'd been distracted.

He'd turned to leave and Bubba the pimp had conked him on the head. While it hadn't knocked him out as intended—he was a vampire, after all—the blow had sent a blast of pain through Jake that was so intense he'd actually forgotten the damnable need to feed. He'd forgotten everything except the pressure beating at his skull.

He'd turned and Bubba had hit him again, and Jake had let him. Over and over. Until the hurt had obliterated everything and he'd stopped thinking altogether.

"This ass-whipping didn't have anything to do with that sweet little piece you were keeping time with back at the community center, did it?"

A sweet vision pushed into his throbbing head and eased the ache just a little. "Her name is Nikki."

"Ah, Nikki. I'm judging by the way you look ready to jump me for calling her a *piece* that it has everything to do with her. Jake, you know you can't do this."

"Do what?"

"Fall for a human."

"I'm not falling for anyone." He'd already fallen. Hard and fast and now the damage was done. "Mind your own business."

"We've been friends a long time. When you need me, I've got your back. When I need you, you've got mine. That's the way it's been for over a hundred years."

"Then you should know I mean it when I tell you to stay out. This doesn't have anything to do with you."

Garret didn't say anything. He simply stared at Jake long and hard, as if trying to figure something out. "This is suicide, you know. In the shape you're in, Sam will be the one staking you, and you know it."

"So?"

"So you have to feed," Garret told him. "Anything can happen when two vampires face off. Especially when one is reliving the turning. You know how crazy things can get." His gaze caught and held Jake's. "How violent. I doubt Sam takes the same precautions that you and I do. Which means you might not make it, buddy."

Maybe not.

And maybe that wouldn't be so bad.

It was a crazy thought. One he quickly squelched. He'd been searching far too long to give up when success was right in front of him. He could see it, smell it, taste it—*freedom.*

An honest-to-goodness future free of the curse.

A normal life.

The thing was, Jake wasn't so sure he wanted one. Not if he had to live it without Nikki Braxton.

NIKKI HATED HER LIFE.

She came to that conclusion on Saturday afternoon as she popped the side of her computer with the palm of her hand and watched the wave of colors on the screen. She popped it again.

"You're going to break it," Charlie said as he turned off the power plug at his station. It wasn't closing time yet, but he was heading home early to pick up Darlene for the rodeo finale that night.

Likewise, Nikki had finished up her last cut and color ten minutes ago. She'd given herself a lighter schedule on purpose because she'd expected to spend Saturday night with Jake.

She smacked the computer again. "Dill was supposed to fix this."

"He fixed the actual computer itself. That looks like the monitor. Call him again." Charlie stared through the front windows at the shop across the street. "He hasn't closed up yet."

She picked up the phone, ranted at Dill for a few minutes before guilt got the best of her and she apologized. "I'm sorry. I've just had a tough day," she told him, waving at him through the window. "I don't mean to be a bee-yotch."

"It's okay. Mrs. Weston called me a four-eyes when she picked up her PDA at lunch. I had to delete her schedule when I reloaded software. I gave her a printout, but that wasn't good enough."

Nikki's guilt multiplied. "I'm sure she didn't mean it."

"Oh, she meant it all right. But it's okay. I've been called worse, that's for sure. So you're sure it's the monitor? It could be the motherboard. It looked like it was on its last legs when I replaced those circuits. But you never know with motherboards. It could last a few days or a few years. It's better to wait until it screws up completely."

"Trust me, it's screwed."

"I'm working on something right now, but I'll stop by just as soon as I finish. It might be a half hour to an hour."

"Take your time. I don't have any plans."

"Trouble in paradise?" Charlie asked as he glanced at tomorrow's schedule.

"There is no paradise. We broke up."

"You're kidding, right?" Nikki shook her head and Charlie added, "But just last night you looked so happy."

"That's the way it goes. One day everything's stored nice and neat in the closet and the next it's all hanging out."

"Don't tell me you caught him trying on your underwear?"

She shook her head.

"Your shoes?"

Another shake.

"He borrowed your lipstick, didn't he?"

"It's nothing like that. He…he's just not the man I thought, that's all."

Not yet.

The notion echoed in her head as she slapped the computer one more time before killing the power.

"Don't do it," Charlie told her when she leaned over to unplug the power cord.

"I have to unplug it. How else is Dill supposed to pick it up?"

"I'm not talking about the computer. I'm talking about Jake." Her friend gave her a knowing look. "You've been the happiest I've ever seen you this past week. Dingy but happy. No guy's ever gotten to you like this, and now you're trying to push him away."

"I have good reason to push him away."

"Really? What? Is he an ex-con? A serial killer? A woman stuck in a man's body?"

"No."

"Then you have no reason to push Jake away the way you've pushed every other guy in your past."

"I don't push guys away."

"Are you kidding me? You push harder than a steamroller. Come on, Nikki. Stop for once. Break the cycle."

"I do not have a cycle."

"Like hell you don't. You're a pervert magnet."

"Excuse me?"

"You purposely attract men with all these deep, dark, weird secrets. Guys who are obviously holding back. Everybody in the free world can see these guys have issues—except you." He leveled a gaze at her. "Then again, I think you see it just like everybody else. It's what attracts you to them. You attract guys who hold back because you hold back. The closer you get, the more you realize these men aren't what you thought they were and so you bail. Before," he added, "you let them see the real you. See, they open up, but you don't. You turn tail and run before then. You do it on purpose because you're afraid of a real relationship. You're afraid to just be yourself."

"Don't you have a wife to go home to?"

"I'm going, but you mark my words. You're making a mistake with this guy."

"You don't know him. He's not the man for me." He wasn't a man, period. Even so, it would be much too easy to fall for him.

She couldn't do that and then say goodbye.

She wouldn't.

JAKE'S EYES POPPED open and his gaze darted around the cave. Garret still slept the sleep of the dead several feet away, his head propped on his saddlebags, his hands folded across his chest. He wore only his jeans and a peaceful expression.

Jake's gaze skittered to the waterfall. It drip-dropped, keeping time with the frantic beat of his heart.

He'd had the dream again.

The hair on his arms tickled and his pulse raced. Awareness zipped up and down his spine.

Sam was here.

The confrontation was over twenty-four hours away, but that didn't make Jake any less anxious. The dream had been too vivid. Too deadly.

He pulled on his clothes and boots and climbed onto his motorcycle. The engine roared, cracking open the silence and bringing Garret wide-awake.

Jake met his friend's gaze, but the vampire didn't say anything. He read the anxiety fueling Jake and he mistook it for the hunger.

But what drove Jake was far more powerful than the hunger for blood or sex.

Worry and fear whirled together, snaking around him and pulling tight.

He wound his way through the cave, dread building by

the second. He emerged into the clearing just as dusk settled in. Gray shadows crowded the trees, making them seem darker as Jake steered deeper into the forest. When he broke free, he hit the dirt road at a frenzied speed, pushing the bike faster until he was running wide open. Desperate.

She had to be okay.

She just had to be.

CHARLIE DIDN'T HAVE a clue about Nikki's love life.

That's what she told herself as she headed home. She tried to pull it off like any other Saturday night. She stopped to pick up pizza. She even bought a pint of ice cream for dessert. But no amount of pepperoni or Chocolate Ecstasy could distract her from the sound of Charlie's voice, which stuck in her head.

Afraid? She wasn't afraid to be herself. She was just afraid to get close to someone who would surely break her heart. Jake was temporary. That was the real problem. It wasn't her. Charlie was a hairdresser, not Dr. Phil, and she didn't—repeat, did *not*—have a cycle.

No, what she had was a very tormented vampire standing at her front door.

He wore faded jeans, a simple white T-shirt and a relieved expression.

"You're okay," he said when she opened the front door, as if the fact surprised him.

What did he expect? For her to be drowning her sorrows in a gallon of Cookie Dough ice cream? She glanced down at the spoon in her hand and quickly shoved it behind her back. "I'm fine. Never better."

"I'm glad." But he didn't look it. Rather, he looked tired, worn. She noted the tight lines around his mouth and the shadows beneath his eyes. The faint line of a cut marred his usually perfect forehead.

She couldn't stop herself. She reached out, her fingers flitting over the scratch. "What happened?"

He closed his eyes for a brief moment, as if relishing her touch, and it took every ounce of strength she had to pull away.

"I had a run-in with a baseball bat," he said as her hand fell to her side.

"You got *hit* with a bat?"

"This is nothing." His mouth hinted at a grin and her heart hammered in response. "You should have seen me last night. It's no big deal. I heal pretty quickly." A serious light touched his eyes. "One of the perks of being a vampire." He stared at her as if he wanted to say more, but then he seemed to think better of it. "I just wanted to make sure you were okay." He started to turn away, but then he stopped himself. "And to tell you something."

"What?"

"I didn't drink from you—" his gaze met hers "—but I wanted to. I wanted it so bad. I've never felt that way with any woman. It's either the sex or the blood. Never both. Until you." And then he turned away.

Let him go, she told herself. *Let him go and forget him just like every other man in your past.*

Every.

Single.

One.

Oh, no.

The truth crystallized as she watched Jake walk away from her, his back stiff, as if it took every ounce of strength he had to put one foot in front of the other.

Charlie had been right about her.

She'd spent a lifetime being afraid to open up, to really let anyone close to her because she feared that they wouldn't really and truly like her for who she was deep down inside. A bona fide good girl or bad to the bone? She didn't know.

She only knew one thing—she loved Jake.

And while she might be better off in the long run by turning her back now, suddenly the future didn't matter half as much as her desperation to act on that love and break the cycle once and for all.

"Jake!"

17

HER DESPERATE VOICE echoed in Jake's ears and stopped him cold.

He turned to see Nikki poised in the doorway. She wore an ugly pair of sweatpants and a big, bulky sweatshirt—and she couldn't have looked more beautiful. Her eyes glittered a deep, vibrant gold, and desperation worried her expression.

"Don't go."

Her plea crossed the distance to him, and in the blink of an eye he stood before her. But he didn't reach out and touch her. He couldn't and she knew it.

She knew him. The man. The vampire.

"Why don't you come inside for a little while?"

It was the invitation he'd been waiting for, yet he didn't act on it. He could have. He could have thrown her over his shoulder, carted her inside the house, up the stairs and straight to bed.

That's what he yearned to do.

He held himself steady and stared deep into her eyes. "Why?"

"I…" She caught her full bottom lip to stop its trembling. "I acted really awful last night, but I was scared."

He stiffened. "Of me," he stated flatly.

She shook her head. "Of myself. But I'm not anymore. I know you want to be with me. You need me." Meaning gleamed in her bright gaze. "And I need you. I want to be with you tonight. All night."

"And tomorrow?"

"We'll worry about that when the time comes." She leveled a stare at him, and he saw the sincerity gleaming in her eyes. "Okay?" Her voice was small, as if she was actually afraid he might turn and walk away.

As if he could ever do such a thing.

She was offering him the most precious gift in the world. Her body. Her blood.

Her heart.

That's what he wanted. At the same time, he knew it would only make walking away that much harder. If he walked away.

Before he could dwell on the possibility, he stepped forward and backed her up into the house.

Turning, he closed and locked the door and then backed her up another few steps toward the wall. A sense of urgency rushed through him and he grasped the hem of her shirt. He pulled it up and over her head and tossed it to the hardwood floor. His fingers went to the clasp of her bra and her breasts spilled free.

He dipped his head and drew one sensitive peak into his mouth. She tasted every bit as good as he remembered. More so because there were no secrets between them. He didn't have to be afraid of her, and she didn't have to be afraid of him, and he meant to prove that once and for all.

Nikki closed her eyes against the wonderful pull of Jake's mouth on her breast. He sucked her so hard and so thoroughly and she sagged against him. Wetness flooded the sensitive flesh between her legs and drenched her panties. He drew on her harder, his jaw creating a powerful tug that she felt clear to her womb. An echoing throb started in her belly, more intense with every rasp of his tongue, every nibble of his teeth....

The thought faded as she felt the razorlike sharpness against her sensitive flesh. Her body went stiff and he pulled away.

She opened her eyes and found herself staring up at him the way he'd been their first night together.

He stared down at her, into her, his eyes hot and vivid, his fangs fully visible. He didn't move. Rather, he waited, his body taut, his muscles stretched tight.

She trailed her hand along his jaw, touched his bottom lip and smiled. And then she snaked her arms around his neck and pulled him back down to her breast.

That was all the urging he needed. He suckled her, laving, grazing, driving her to the brink of insanity. But he didn't bite her. Not yet.

No matter how much she suddenly wanted him to.

Heat flowered through her, pulsing along her nerve endings, heating her body until she felt as if she would explode.

He didn't touch her with his hands. Just his mouth. He worked her until she moaned long and low and deep in her throat and her nipple throbbed. Goose bumps chased up and down her arms, and her legs trembled.

"Please," she murmured.

He seized the other nipple and delivered the same delicious torture. She grew wetter, hotter, her body shivering with each movement of his mouth.

And then his mouth was on hers, his hot fingers rolling and plucking her damp nipples. She felt the sharpness of his fangs against her lips, and the sensation sent a shiver of excitement through her.

He pulled her flush against him, his hands trailing down her bare back, stirring every nerve ending along the way. Fingers played at her waistband before slipping lower. His palms cupped her buttocks through the material. He urged her up on her tiptoes until her pelvis cradled the massive erection straining beneath his zipper.

The feel of him sent a burst of longing through her and suddenly she couldn't get close enough. She grasped his shoulders and clutched at his T-shirt as she wrapped one leg around his thigh. His erection rubbed against her slit and she moaned. She couldn't get enough of him, kissing him with all of the passion that had built inside her.

He tugged at the elastic waistband of her sweats and pushed at the material until it slid over her hips, her thighs, to puddle around her ankles. His fingers snagged on the straps of her panties and urged them down. Until she was completely naked.

He slid his hand between her legs and played the slick flesh. His thumb grazed her clitoris, rasping back and forth, over and over. She bucked as delicious tremors racked her body.

She was so lost in the throes of her orgasm that she

didn't even notice that he'd picked her up and carted her up the stairs until she felt the soft mattress at her back.

She glanced up in time to see him peel off his shirt and unfasten his jeans. He shoved the denim down in one smooth motion, his erection springing forward, huge and greedy. A white drop of pearly liquid oozed from the ripe purple head and slithered down his strong length. She couldn't help herself. She scrambled to her knees, leaned forward and caught the drop with the tip of her tongue.

He groaned, long and low and deep, his fingers splaying in her hair, cradling her head as she licked him from root to tip and back down again. He tasted salty and sweet and she couldn't seem to get enough.

"Not yet," he finally croaked. "I want to be inside you when I come. I want to feel you hot and tight around me." He pushed her into the mattress, urged her legs apart and settled his erection flush against her sex.

He kissed her then, licking her lips and sucking at her tongue before he caught her bottom and tilted her just so. With one powerful thrust he slid inside her.

Her head fell back and her eyes closed and her body convulsed around him.

"Look at me, Nikki." His deep, raw voice drew her eyes open and she stared up at him.

Hunger blazed hot and intense in his gaze as he opened his mouth. His fangs glittered in the moonlight as he poised above her and waited.

He was giving her one last chance to bail. He'd opened the closet door and unleashed the monster that lived and breathed inside.

"For now," his deep voice reminded her. *"For tonight."*

She arched her body and tilted her head, baring her neck, offering it to him. She knew what he needed if he intended to succeed and she meant to do everything to help him.

Even more, she wanted this connection with him. She wanted to take all that he offered and give everything she had in return.

No more holding back.

He dipped his head. His mouth closed over the side of her neck where her pulse beat a frantic rhythm. He licked the spot, teasing and tasting, and then he sank his fangs deep. So deep. Oddly enough, it didn't hurt. Just a stirring prickle, and then she felt a pleasure so intense her mouth fell open and a gasp trembled from her throat.

And then the real pleasure started.

He thrust into her, pushing deep with his body, all the while drawing with his mouth. He drove her mindless, pushing and drawing, giving and taking, over and over. The pressure inside of her built, climbing higher until she couldn't take anymore. She cried out, splintering into a thousand pieces.

His entire body seemed to vibrate as she came apart. He trembled and buzzed, drinking in her power-infusing blood as he drank in the sexual energy that rushed from her body like a tidal wave gunning for shore.

His mouth eased and he leaned back. A fierce groan rumbled from his lips as he thrust one final time and followed her over the edge. His body shook with the force of his climax as he collapsed on top of her, his arms braced on either side of her head, his face buried in the crook of her neck.

A few frantic heartbeats later, he rolled onto his back, pulling her on top of him without breaking their contact. He held her tight, as if he feared she might slip away.

Nikki felt weightless, almost dizzy. She rested her head on his shoulder and drank in several deep draughts of air. A tiny trickle of warmth slid down her collarbone and she reached up. Her fingertips brushed the two tiny pinpoints where he'd bitten her and a sharp burst of desire knifed through her. She jumped.

Surprised. Startled. Turned on.

"It's only painful if it's meant to be," he told her, his hand coming up to soothe the area. Not that it worked. It only served to stir her up even more. Her nipples pebbled and her thighs clenched and she closed her eyes as warmth bubbled between her legs and fizzled through her.

"I would never hurt you," he told her as he slid his hand down the length of her body, stroking, soothing. "Never."

"I know that." Her eyelids fluttered open to find him staring up at her. Her gaze met his. "I know you."

Desperation fired in the rich silver depths, along with a fierce determination. He was thinking about the looming confrontation. "Thank you," he murmured after a long, thoughtful moment. *"Thank you."*

"My pleasure," she said—and meant it. She'd never felt such sensation with anyone but Jake. Sure, sex had been all right. But never incredible. Never like this.

Never again.

She fought down a wave of regret, settled her hand over his heart and closed her eyes.

WHEN NIKKI WOKE on Sunday morning, she yawned and stretched and basked in the afterglow of their incredible lovemaking for all of five seconds before reality set in.

Tonight was *the* night.

When the clock struck midnight, Jake would face off with Sam. And afterward he would ride out of Skull Creek and never look back.

He loves you, a voice whispered. *He won't leave.*

Nikki wanted to think so, but she kept remembering all the times Jolene had stumbled in late at night and bypassed her daughter's room. There'd been no good-night kiss. No hugs. Nothing. Because while Jolene had, indeed, loved Nikki, she'd loved herself more. She'd been more concerned with her own wants and desires. Her own needs.

Jake needed his freedom. He'd fought too long and too hard to simply give it up over a little thing like love.

If he did, indeed, love her.

He'd never said the words.

He couldn't. Jake didn't make promises he couldn't keep and so he'd kept his mouth shut.

Because after tonight, he was leaving, whether he loved her or not.

If he succeeded.

And if he didn't? He wouldn't be going anywhere because he would be dead.

Either way, Nikki faced a future without Jake McCann.

NIKKI SPENT HER ENTIRE morning trying not to think about Jake. She threw herself into painting the kitchen. From the walls to the cabinets. Every time she started to think, she worked that much faster, making long, swift strokes here, dabbing there, until she finished. She rinsed out her brushes then, determined to stay busy and avoid the dread that built with each passing moment.

She'd just washed and put away the last brush when she heard the knock on the door.

For a few frantic heartbeats she actually entertained the notion that her life wasn't some crazy nightmare. That Jake was just a man and he was here right now, ring in hand, ready to plop down on one knee and breathe life into her happily ever after.

The small thread of hope that blossomed as Nikki walked from the kitchen to the front door quickly died when she found Aunt Izzie and Jolene standing on the other side.

"You didn't make it to church," Izzie pointed out. "It was your turn to bring the coffee cake for the Sunday school."

"I've been painting."

"I guess it was too much to hope that you'd had a late night with that boyfriend of yours and had finally decided to sleep in," Jolene said.

"Jolene Marie Braxton, that's an obscene thing to say," Izzie huffed.

Jolene eyed her aunt. "What's obscene is the number of coffee cakes you old biddies consume in the name of religion. Why, I'm sure they didn't have coffee cake at the Lord's supper. Now wine—"

"The disciples drank wine as a symbol, not for personal pleasure."

"And you would know because you're old enough to have been there, right?"

"You have no shame."

"And you have far too much."

"Come and see the kitchen," Nikki blurted before the argument could get any more heated. She turned and led both women through a maze of boxes, toward the kitchen. She turned as they entered the freshly painted space and motioned around her. "So what do you think?"

Izzie looked both surprised and dismayed. "I figured you would go with one color."

"Me, too." Jolene's gaze went from one cabinet to the next. "What happened to the red?"

"It's red."

"Just the trim." Jolene frowned. "You should have gone completely red."

"It's a kitchen, not a bordello," Izzie said, her own gaze sweeping the walls. "She should have gone with the yellow."

"Yellow is blah, and nobody says *bordello* anymore. The PC term is *whorehouse*."

"Oh, just hush," Izzie told Jolene. Her gaze shifted back to the cabinets. "Solid yellow would have been so much more cheerful, dear."

"Solid red is much more interesting."

"I really like them both," Nikki blurted.

She did, she realized as she stared at the pale yellow cabinets trimmed in vibrant cherry. The combination was both bright and bold. Peaceful yet daring. A little bit good, at the same time, a little bit bad.

And that was okay.

Even more, that was Nikki.

The truth hit as she stood listening to her mother and

aunt debate the merits of the two different paint colors. The same way they debated everything, from how much makeup Nikki should wear and what type of clothes to which dessert to have or what television shows to watch.

They sat on opposite sides of the spectrum when it came to life, and Nikki had spent thirty years swinging from one end to the other. Trying to be bad enough for one yet good enough for the other. She'd been caught in between, eager to be loved by both, feeling all the while unloved by either.

But she was loved.

Jake loved her. She'd seen it in his eyes. Felt it in his touch.

Whether he went or stayed, he *did* love her.

All of her, from the bold, bad woman who'd taken her pleasure on the Ferris wheel to the kind, conservative woman who donated her services at the retirement home every Sunday.

He loved the fact that Nikki was a little bit bad *and* a little bit good.

She *was* both, and suddenly that didn't seem like such a bad thing.

"The yellow's nice," Nikki told the two older women, "but it's too bland without the red to spice it up. Likewise, the red needs the yellow or it's just too much. It's the perfect combination of both—and so am I."

"I beg your pardon?" Izzie arched a questioning brow.

"Me. I'm the perfect combination of the two of you. I've got Mom's flair for fashion," she told Izzie, "and I like showing off a little skin once in a while."

"Nicole Elizabeth—"

"On the other hand," she cut in, turning toward Jolene,

"I don't flash my goodies in everybody's face just for the hell of it." She caught her mother's gaze and held steady. "That's not me, Mom. I know that's what you want me to be, but I'm not." Her gaze shifted to Izzie. "And I'm not a saint, either. I'm not even close. And I don't want to be. I know you might not want to hear that, but that's the way it is. It's the way I am, take it or leave it."

They left it.

Izzie's mouth dropped open and Jolene's gaze flashed disappointment, and then both women walked out without so much as a goodbye. And it was okay.

It was all okay.

Because Nikki Braxton was through trying to please other people. From here on out, the only person she wanted to please was herself.

It was no longer about what everyone else wanted. No, it was about what *she* wanted.

And she wanted Jake.

She wanted him to win tonight. To stay tomorrow. She wanted the next fifty years with him.

If only he wanted the same.

He didn't. She knew it and so she tried to tell herself to forget him. To get on with her life.

Better to have loved and lost than never to have loved at all.

She held tight to the thought and went about her usual Sunday.

She went by the hardware store to pick out colors for the living room—a neutral beige with a bold navy-blue trim—before heading over to the retirement home.

She spent the rest of the day doing perms, mixing hair color and listening to the latest gossip. But that's where the usual ended. The Greyhounds were too eager to talk about Jake, and so she begged off poker with them in favor of catching up on all the things she'd neglected at the salon.

She unpacked and counted hair care products, replaced the old magazines with the new and restocked the individual stations with everything from hair spray to highlighting foil.

But no matter how busy she kept herself, it wasn't enough to distract her from the foreboding that sat in the pit of her stomach and gained momentum as darkness fell.

A feeling that had nothing to do with the fact that Jake was leaving tomorrow and everything to do with tonight and the impending confrontation.

Something was wrong.

She knew it even before she saw the man standing on the other side of the front glass door of her salon.

He looked like any other biker, with his bandanna and his skull-and-crossbones T-shirt. But she knew better because she'd seen the other side of him.

Just as she'd seen Jake.

"There's something about you," he said, his voice as loud and as clear as if he stood right in front of her rather than several feet away, a wall of glass and a dead-bolt lock between them. "You've got energy."

"Is that the classic vampire pickup line?"

He grinned. "I'm not trying to pick you up. Jake's my buddy. I wouldn't do that to him." His gaze grew serious. "I'm worried about him, though. About tonight."

"What's wrong?"

"Nothing. Yet." He shook his head. "When a vampire is reliving his turning, he's extremely powerful. Invincible. *Deadly.* I don't know if Jake is up for this."

Panic bolted through her, followed by a whirlwind of dread. "You can help him, can't you? You have to help him."

"Actually, you're the one who can help." He leveled a stare at her. "If you're interested."

"What can I do?"

He glanced at the locked door. "You can start by letting me in. Talking loudly through all this glass isn't the smartest thing. The last thing we need is for Sam to overhear what we're up to."

He was right. She knew that, but she hesitated anyway.

Duh. He was a vampire. A bloodsucker. A creature of the night.

While she trusted Jake not to hurt her, what did she know of the rest of his kind?

At the same time, this wasn't just any vampire. This was Jake's friend, and he needed her help.

She had a sudden vision of Jake lying somewhere, a stake through his heart, and she stepped forward. Throwing the dead bolt, she pulled open the door and Garret Sawyer walked into her shop.

"How can I help?" She shut the door behind him.

"First off, Jake needs to feed."

"He fed last night."

"It's not enough." Garret shook his head. "The more he feeds, the more powerful he is." His gaze went to her neck. "Are you up for this?"

"Of course." She touched a hand to the faint bruises that still remained. The tiny prick points had healed with remarkable speed. By tomorrow there would be no trace that Jake had ever touched her, much less drunk from her essence. A prickle of regret went through her, followed by renewed determination. "I'll do everything I can."

"I'll take you to him, then, and you can feed him again."

She nodded and turned to retrieve her purse. She'd just grabbed the leather strap when she felt his presence behind her. "I'm ready," she said as she turned.

"So am I." He stood right behind her, so close he almost touched her. But he didn't.

Not with his hands.

But his eyes… They reached out, beckoning to her, pulling her in.

In a trembling moment Nikki realized that this was what Jake had been talking about when he'd said that vampires had the power to entrance humans. To mesmerize them until they were weak and willing and…

No!

She summoned her strength and steeled herself against the strange look in his gaze, but it was too late.

The floor trembled and her legs shook, and then she felt herself crumble. And then the darkness closed in.

18

"YOU DO LOVE HIM."

The voice sounded in Nikki's ears the moment she forced her eyes open. Her head throbbed and her back hurt. Her mouth tasted gritty, her tongue thick. She blinked, willing her eyes to adjust to the darkness and the figure who loomed over her, blocking out what little bit of moonlight pushed into the deserted barn.

Scratchy rope wound around her ankles and pulled tight. But not too tight. She could still feel her toes. Rough fingers rasped against the bare skin of her feet as the shadow looped strands and fastened them together.

Seconds ticked by as she struggled to remember the past moments, but it was too dark and her head hurt too much.

"Try to keep your eyes open and the dizziness will fade." The shadow spoke again, the voice faintly familiar.

In a rush, memories flooded her. Garret's unexpected visit to her salon. Her invitation for him to come in. Their discussion about Jake and—

Garret.

"You've got it bad," he added. "Otherwise you would still be out of it." He finished the last knot, sat back on his haunches and tugged to test his handiwork.

"What did you do to me?" Her voice sounded gravelly at first, but with each word her lips started to feel like her own once again.

"It's called a trance. And it usually has a lot more staying power. But since you're hooked on Jake, you're resistant to my charms." He shrugged. "I thought that might be the case when I saw how broken up he was last night." He tugged on the ropes again. "That's what these are for."

"I thought you were his friend."

"I am." A tortured light touched his eyes, as if he warred deep inside himself. Good versus evil. Enemies against friends. "But self-preservation comes first. I can't let him show up for the turning. I won't."

"It's you," Nikki said as the full meaning of his words hit her. "*You're* Sam Black."

"I was. A long, long time ago." He shook his head. "Then I was Sam Sawyer. Then Billy Black. And now I'm Garret Sawyer. It's a vampire's way. We have to protect our true nature and so we change. People die. Vampires change their names."

"But you're a hero." It was stupid thing to say, but it was all that popped into her brain at that moment. She was still reeling from the truth. Garret was Sam Black. *The* Sam Black.

"I was no such thing." He looked almost wistful when he spoke, the words laced with regret. "I was just a lucky kid defending my home. My people." He shook his head and the tortured light returned. Pain laced his words. "I was lucky, all right. Then my luck ran out." He stiffened as he seemed to realize that he'd said too much. "I'm no hero. I'm a vampire. Remember that."

"Why are you doing this?"

"To keep Jake out of the way so I can do what I have to do. If he's busy looking for you—and he will be because the two of you are linked now—then he won't confront me. He'll never know who I am."

"He won't give up his chance at humanity to look for me." Even as she said the words, she knew she was wrong. He would come after her just as Garret predicted—and he would miss his chance at redemption.

"If he comes looking for me, I'll tell him it's you. He'll go after you."

"Then we'll face off if...when the time comes. But not now."

"Why not just kill me?" The words were out before she could stop them. *Idiot,* a voice whispered. *Don't go giving him ideas.*

But she knew that killing her wasn't a possibility he hadn't already thought of. For whatever reason, he'd chosen not to act on it. She could see it in the firm but gentle way he checked the ropes on her ankles. He reached up and tested her hands.

"It's really tight."

He didn't look as if he believed her, but she made a big show of wincing and he worked at the knots. The ties loosened just a hair.

"Better?" His gaze found hers.

"Thank you." She watched as he pushed to his feet and walked around the barn, checking windows to make sure the shutters were firmly in place. "Why don't you just kill him? Then you wouldn't spend the rest of eternity looking over your shoulder. You did it once."

"I didn't mean—" he started, but then he shook his head.

"You didn't mean what? To kill him? You're a vampire. That's what you do."

He paused, his hand on one shutter, and he stiffened. "Trying to talk me into it, are you? Maybe you don't care for him as much as he thinks you do."

But she did care about Jake.

And so did Garret.

"He'll kill you," she told him.

"I have no doubt. Why do you think I'm going to all this trouble?" He walked toward her. "I don't want to kill Jake, but I don't want him to kill me, either." He reached into his saddlebags and pulled out a roll of tape. Tearing off a piece, he leaned toward her.

"You don't have to do—" The tape covered her mouth and all that came out was a squeal.

"The longer it takes him to find you, the better. The turning will be over and I'll be gone by then."

And if not?

Jake would kill him. She knew it. She felt it.

As much as she suddenly disliked Garret, she couldn't let Jake do that. Not because she cared for the traitorous vampire. No, she cared for Jake. No way would he be able to live with himself if he killed Garret Sawyer.

Because Jake wasn't a killer.

He might be a vampire, but he wasn't cold or ruthless or any of those things. He cared about people. He cared about her. And he cared about Garret.

She closed her eyes and called out to him.

SAM HAD NIKKI.

Jake knew it even before her desperate voice rushed through his head just an hour before midnight.

It was a ploy. A trick to lure him away from the square. He'd suspected Sam might use her ever since he'd had the first dream, and the voice now was proof.

She was okay. Last night, their connection increased tenfold. The bond was now solid. Unbreakable. He would have sensed pain. Rather, he felt her frenzy. Her anxiety. She was eager to get free, but she was unharmed.

Soon, he sent her the silent promise. *I'll come for you soon.*

He fought the urge to go to her and blocked out her frantic calls. Time was a luxury now, and he had too much riding on the confrontation to risk being even a second late.

His future waited for him. A future filled with sunlight and Nikki.

He gripped the edge of the rocks and pulled his dripping body from the spring. In minutes he was dry and dressed and ready. He pulled the stake from his saddlebags and hooked it in the back waistband of his pants. He spared a glance at the empty bedroll nearby. Garret had promised to meet him in town. Jake had no doubt he was probably feeding, strengthening himself so that he could help with the confrontation. He needn't bother. Jake wasn't going to let Garret fight his battles. He was going to scope out the area and keep his eyes open. He wouldn't be a sitting duck.

Climbing on the bike, he turned the key and kicked the starter. The engine caught, roaring to life in a puff of noise and smoke. Kicking the gear, Jake sent the bike roaring from the cave, headed straight for town.

It was time.

IT'S ME, DAMMIT. Nikki sent the thought out to Jake, but it was useless. She didn't hear his deep soothing voice in her head. Nothing since he'd sent her the first message. For whatever reason, he was tuning her out.

She fought down a wave of aggravation and struggled against the ropes. They pushed and pulled, but they didn't give. She scooted to the left, searching for something—anything—to saw through the ropes. Other than a sprinkling of hay here and there, there was nothing. The barn had obviously been deserted for quite some time.

Struggling toward the door, she rocked flat on her back and pulled up her knees. She was just about to kick the door as hard as she could when something flashed in her peripheral vision.

She turned her head to the side in time to see Dillon Cash peer inside one of the windows. His gaze landed on her and relief swept through her.

"It's okay," he whispered. "I'm going to get you out of here."

A few seconds later, she heard a dull thud on the outside of the door. Metal scraped and wood cracked and the door popped open.

"I think I love you," she blurted when he pulled the tape from her mouth. When a blush darkened his face, she added, "I'm speaking figuratively, Dill. I'm just really glad to see you. What are you doing here?"

"I was working late and I saw your lights on in the salon." He pushed the thick glasses back up onto the bridge of his nose and pulled a small knife from his pocket of tools. He started sawing at the ropes that bound her hands. "I figured I would drop your computer off so you'd have it for tomorrow morning. I was just about to leave my place when I saw you with that guy. You looked funny. Almost drugged. I got worried, so I followed you."

"What time is it?"

"Almost eleven-thirty."

"But we left the salon at barely nine o'clock. What took you so long?"

"I was following you, but then I lost you. He was driving that motorcycle really fast. Anyhow, I didn't see him turn off until he was coming back toward town. Alone. I saw him turn onto the main road, so I backtracked down the farm road and retraced his steps." His glasses slid down the bridge of his nose again and he pushed them back up. "I figured he'd dumped you in a ditch somewhere, so I drove really slow." He finished cutting through her ropes and her hands broke free. He went to work on the ankle ropes next. "We should hurry in case he comes back."

"He's not coming back," she told him as he freed her ankles. She rubbed the feeling back into her hands and tried to stand.

Dill reached out to help her up. "Can you walk?"

"Don't worry about me." She was already moving toward the doorway. "We have to get back to town."

"I'll take you straight to the police station."

"No."

"The hospital?"

She shook her head. "The square." She followed him out to his truck and climbed into the passenger seat. Her gaze fell to the clock on the dash and a wave of panic swept through her. "Fast!"

"GO HOME," SHE TOLD Dill once they'd reached Main Street. He idled near the curb several yards away from the entrance to the square.

"But we have to report this guy—"

"No. Listen, there's something else going on. You can't call the police. You can't call anyone. Just go home and I'll call you tomorrow." When he looked hesitant, she added, "I really appreciate what you did. Please, Dill. Trust me. Just go." He finally nodded and shifted his truck into drive.

Nikki slammed the door and started for the square at a full run.

She was just a few yards shy of the entrance when someone grabbed her from behind.

JAKE STOOD IN THE shadow of the courthouse and stared across the square. The shadows seemed to come from out of nowhere. A man and a woman. A struggle.

"You're not supposed to be here." Garret's voice carried the distance and slid into Jake's ears.

Garret?

Denial rushed through Jake as he watched the man pick up the woman and move effortlessly toward the shadows.

Jake knew it was Nikki even before he heard her frantic

"Let go!" He felt the sudden change from panic to full-blown fear. "I won't let you hurt him," she cried.

The truth crystallized as Jake's gaze skittered to the small portable cooler that sat nearby. Even before he popped open the top, he knew the contents. Bags from the blood bank back in Houston. Blood to quench the wild thirst during the turning. His stare riveted on the struggling couple and he *knew*.

He reached them in a split second. He slammed into Garret from behind and sent him flying. Nikki fell to the ground and scrambled backward. Jake glanced at her, his gaze roving over from head to toe for a fast, furious heart-beat before he turned.

Garret had struggled upright, but he hadn't recovered enough to launch a counterattack.

Jake quickly understood why.

Garret's neck arched, the muscles stretched taut as his head fell back. His body strained and a growl vibrated through the dark night. He stumbled backward, lost in the throes of the turning as the hunger gripped him, turning him from a man to a monster.

Jake lunged, slamming into Garret's body. He fell backward and Jake straddled him. The pain of betrayal ripped through him, making his hands shake as he reached for the stake. He held it high, ready to plunge it deep into the vampire's chest.

"Don't." The word was barely audible. A gasp that crackled with both pain and ecstasy. The fierce red eyes cooled in the next instant as Garret stared up at Jake. "I—I'm sorry."

"It doesn't matter."

But it did.

Images rushed at him, and he saw Garret leaning over him, offering his own blood to help ease Jake's hunger until his sanity returned and he could teach him how to feed without losing himself. Garret had saved Jake and taught him how to survive.

Because he'd condemned him in the first place.

The truth raged inside Jake, urging him to push the stake deep, to end Garret's miserable existence.

"You did this to me," Jake snarled, baring his fangs. A growl shook his vocal cords. "You took my soul."

"I didn't mean to," Garret ground out, closing his eyes, his face clenched tight against the hunger that gripped his body and fought for control. "I couldn't help it. I was just like you…fighting who I was…what I was… I resisted, but then it turned the tables on me and kicked my ass. I was crazed and hungry and…" He gritted his teeth as a convulsion gripped his body. His head fell back and he arched his neck. Veins bulged and a hiss slid past his lips. "I…" Another hiss and he shook his head. "I—I couldn't stop myself. When the hunger passed, you were dead. It was either leave you that way or turn you, so I let you drink from me." His eyes opened then and he stared up at Jake. "I took your life from you. I had to give it back."

"You didn't give me my life back. You gave me hell. *Hell.*"

Even as he said the words, he wasn't so sure he believed them. Not when the past few days with Nikki had felt more like heaven. When they were together, he felt happy. Content. Hopeful.

He'd thought for so long that killing was the only means to save himself. When all along all he'd had to do was fall in love.

"Jake." Her pleading voice filled his ears. "Don't. Don't do something you'll regret. You're not like him."

But that's where she was wrong. He craved the blood just as fiercely. He always would.

"He's your friend." He felt her hand on his, urging the stake away. "You don't want to do this."

He didn't.

Garret Sawyer *was* his best friend. The older vampire might have turned him out of guilt and he might even have taken Jake under his wing because of that same guilt. But over the years they'd developed a bond. Friendship. Trust.

Hope warred with the truth—that Jake couldn't bring himself to hurt Garret. No matter how the vampire had hurt him.

"Don't ever lie to me again," he growled before he eased Garret down to the ground. "The cooler," he told Nikki. "Grab the cooler. He needs to feed. Now. Before the hunger overwhelms him and he loses it—"

"Don't touch her."

Jake turned to find himself staring at the pointy end of the tiniest Phillips screwdriver he'd ever seen.

"Dillon?" It was Nikki's voice. "I told you to go home."

"And leave you to get ripped to shreds? No way." The young man's chest heaved, his mouth sucking huge draughts of air. His gaze zigzagged between Garret's writhing form and Jake. His eyes widened with fear and disbelief. "You've got fangs," he told Jake.

"I know this looks weird, Dill," Nikki started.

"Weird?" He shook his head again. "It's crazy. A *vampire. Here.*"

"He's a good vampire," Nikki told him. "So long as you don't make him mad. Holding a screwdriver on him will definitely make him mad."

"Put it down," Jake said, his voice dark and quiet and compelling. The man's gaze locked with his and he saw the fear fade. "Now."

"Please," Nikki added. Her voice seemed to break the spell Jake had cast and the man shook his head again. Determination fired his expression.

"Like hell. You think I'm crazy?" Dillon's head bobbed from side to side again. "I may be a geek, but I'm not a stupid geek. And I'm not a coward. Get away from him, Nikki."

"She's not going anywhere." Jake stepped forward.

"If you think I'm going to leave her here to get her blood sucked, you've got another thing coming."

"I'm not going to suck her blood."

"You got that right. I know how to do more with this screwdriver than just fix computers."

"Stop it." Nikki slid in front of Jake and faced Dillon. "Put the screwdriver down before you hurt yourself—"

A fierce growl drowned out the rest of her words.

Before Jake could blink, a crazed Garret leaped from behind and grabbed Dillon by the neck. And just like that Garret pinned him to a nearby wall and sank his teeth into Dillon's flesh.

Jake rushed forward, but Garret was too fast. Too hungry. He devoured the young man in less than a few seconds and then thrust him aside. Garret stumbled backward as the hunger seemed to ease. Realization hit him as he stared down at Dillon's lifeless body.

"No," he said, the word a raw, defeated sound that rumbled from his bloody lips. He fell to his knees. *"No!"*

"Garret." Jake's voice drew the older vampire's disoriented gaze. "Go. Take the cooler and feed."

"I…" Garret shook his head as if trying to make some sense of what had happened. "I didn't mean to…"

Jake grasped him by the arm. "Control the hunger," he told the vampire, "or it will control you. I'll take care of this." Garret looked hesitant as he stared at the limp body, but then his gaze shifted to Nikki and a hungry light flared in his eyes. He nodded and shrugged away from Jake. He snatched up the portable cooler and disappeared into the night.

"I'm so sorry," Nikki murmured to Dillon as she lifted his head and eased it onto her leg. She glanced up at Jake. Tears swam in her eyes. "This isn't fair. He was just trying to help me."

"It's going to be okay." Jake touched her shoulder. "Let me have him." She turned knowing eyes up at him and he nodded. "Let me have him," he said again.

Jake waited for Nikki to move away and then he knelt down beside the man and did the only thing he could do— he gave him his life back.

He was leaving.

The truth haunted Nikki all through the next day as she went about her normal Monday routine.

But nothing about her life was normal anymore.

Not that it ever had been in the first place.

But she'd pretended for a while.

Still, a dysfunctional relationship with her mother and aunt and a loser cycle when it came to men paled in comparison to the real truth—she was in love with a vampire who had a best friend who was a vampire who'd turned her computer technician, who just happened to be her nail technician's brother, into a vampire.

Unreal.

At the same time, it was very real.

She stared through the windows to Dillon's repair shop. It sat dark and silent. Before sunup, Jake had reassured Nikki that Dillon would be okay and then he'd left her to take the man home.

Nikki hadn't seen him since.

She'd called and she'd gone by Dillon's house, but no one had answered the door. There'd been no sign of Jake, either.

He hadn't left yet.

She could feel him. He was somewhere close. But not for long.

The knowledge sat heavy in her chest as she tried to go through the motions and pretend that everything was okay. Especially around Cheryl Anne. The girl hadn't talked to her brother in a few days and she'd looked somewhat alarmed when she'd discovered that he hadn't opened up shop. Nikki had made up an excuse that she'd seen him out on a date the night before. While Cheryl Anne had been surprised, she'd also been happy.

"Maybe he's finally breaking out of his shell," she'd said. And then she'd called to tell her parents, who'd been even more excited. It seemed that the town had been placing bets on his sexual preference right along with Nikki's.

There was no doubt in anyone's mind anymore, however. Jake had branded her his in more ways than one.

She touched the now-smooth skin of her neck and called out to him again. Uselessly. He wouldn't answer.

Because he was leaving soon.

But not until darkness fell. Which meant she still had time to find him.

JAKE GLANCED AROUND the abandoned service station one last time. He touched a wall and let his gaze linger near the office. He tucked his dream down deep and turned away. And that was when he saw Nikki standing in the shadows.

"What are you doing here?"

"Looking for you. I felt you." Her gaze collided with his. "So that's it? You're just going to walk away?"

"I have to."

"Why?"

He shook his head. "Are you kidding? It didn't happen. I didn't kill Garret. I won't. Which means I'm still a vampire." He turned away, eager to avoid her disappointment. He'd failed her just as much as he'd failed himself. "I'm staying this way unless I can find Garret's sire. Then I can take him out and we're both free." He shook his head. "But that could be a long, long time." He raked a hand through his hair. "Christ, we don't even have a name. No specifics. Nothing."

"You'll find him anyway."

"Don't do this, Nikki."

"Do what?"

"Pretend that everything will be okay. I'm not what you need. I'm no good for you."

"Why? Because you're a vampire?" Before he could answer, she rushed on. "You're also kind and giving and trustworthy. You have more honor and loyalty than any other man I—"

"I'm *not* a man," he cut in. He shook his head as he fought against the urge to reach out to her. To pull her into his arms and never let go. He couldn't do that to her. He wouldn't.

"You don't love me," she stated. "That's it, isn't it? I thought you didn't say the words because you didn't want to hurt me, but that wasn't it, was it? You don't feel anything for me."

His gaze met hers. "Is that what you really believe?" Even as he asked the question, he knew it was as far from the truth as it could be.

Emotion glittered hot and bright in the whiskey depths of her eyes. She knew. Deep down in her soul, where it mattered most. "I believe in you," she told him. "In us."

He wanted so much to latch on to the words. To never let them go. But he couldn't. He couldn't ignore reality because it would only slap him in the face later on. "I can't be the man you need, Nikki. Maybe one day… But maybe not. Right now, I can't give you the morning after or the morning after that." He shook his head. "I can't give you fifty minutes, let alone fifty years."

"Who cares about a measly fifty when I can have forever?"

"What are you saying?"

Her gaze met his, so steady and sure. "That you drank

from me and now it's my turn to drink from you." She crossed the distance to him, leaned up on her tiptoes and touched her lips to his. "I want you, Jake. Now and forever. I want to spend eternity with you. I love you."

Doubt rushed through him, followed by a sense of joy so profound that he knew he could never turn and walk away from her. Not now. Not twenty years from now. Not ever.

What's more, he didn't want to walk away. To run. To keep running.

As he stared into her eyes, he stopped worrying about the uncertainty of his future. As a man or a vampire, he didn't know. He didn't care. A strange sense of peace stole over him, and for the first time in his existence Jake didn't long for his freedom.

Because he already had it.

Real freedom was loving and being loved.

It was right here. It always had been.

"I love you." He said the words he'd felt for so long but refused to acknowledge. "More than anything."

"Then stay with me."

"For better or for worse," he told her as he took her in his arms and held her close.

"I'd say till death do us part, but there's no such thing for us," she murmured as she smiled up at him. "Just life." She touched her lips to his. "An eternity of it."

Epilogue

SOMETHING WAS definitely up.

Dillon Cash stared down at the massive tent of white cotton that sat smack-dab over his groin. He lifted the edge of the sheet and peeked beneath. His penis stood tall and proud and huge.

What the hell?

Sure, he woke up with the occasional boner. He didn't have a girlfriend and he wasn't particularly fond of whacking off, and so he had more than his share of wet dreams.

But this…this was different.

His gaze shifted to the alarm clock perched on the nightstand. Midnight. Only a sliver of moonlight sliced its way past the drapes, into the room. Yet Dillon could see every detail, from the pencil that sat on the corner of his dresser to the cluttered desk covered with leftover computer parts to the silvery spider web that dangled in the far corner—a web so tiny that he'd never noticed it in the daylight, much less in the middle of the night.

The hair on the nape of his neck stood on end as sounds slid into his ears. The hum of the air conditioner. The creak as the wind whispered through the cracks of the house. The soft play of a radio somewhere in the distance. Voices from a late-night talk show.

But the nearest house sat a good quarter mile up the main road.

Denial rushed through him as he swung his legs over the side of the bed and pushed to his feet. He walked over to the window and shoved the drapes aside. He stared at the endless stretch of pasture. He saw a rabbit dart across the lush grass and disappear into the trees.

He blinked and realized that he wasn't wearing his glasses. His hand came up and he whirled. Sure enough, the black wire frames sat on the nightstand in their usual spot. Close enough that he wouldn't bang his head groping for them before he crawled out of bed. He'd worn glasses for over twenty-five years. Since he'd turned four. Doc Wills had said that he would have to wear them for the rest of his life—

The thought slammed to a halt as a memory rushed at him. Nikki. She'd been tied up in the barn and then she'd been attacked by a vampire and then she'd been in the middle of two vampires and then—

Hold it. Just freakin' *hold* it!

A *vampire?*

No such thing, he told himself. It was just a legend. A way to sell movie tickets and Marilyn Manson CDs. They didn't actually exist.

Yet he'd seen one. Up close and personal.

An image rushed at him. A tortured face. Lethal fangs.

Dillon closed his eyes as he remembered the jagged stab of pain. The frantic fight for each breath. The frenzied flash as his life had passed before his eyes.

And then?

Then he'd found himself back in his bedroom with a killer hard-on.

A *vampire?*

The possibility followed him to the dresser, where he stared at his reflection. He definitely had one, but it seemed different. His eyes appeared greener than usual, his muscles bigger, more defined. His hair looked thicker, shinier. The two zits he'd had on his chin were completely gone. As if they'd never existed.

The energy drinks, he told himself. He'd been sucking down Rockstar like it was water, and now it was paying off.

He struck a pose, marveling at the bulge of his biceps. He was definitely sending in before-and-after shots to the manufacturer. He turned and puffed out his chest. Yep, he was sure to win something for this transformation.

Then again...

He opened his mouth and eyed the incisors that gleamed in the moonlight. His gut clenched and a strange tingling vibrated through his body. His image seemed to shimmer and his eyes gleamed a bright, hot purple.

A vampire, all right.

That's what his gut told him. But his head...

No *freakin'* way.

Denial rushed through him, but it couldn't erase the truth. It stared back at him, and he could no more ignore it than he could have turned down Susie Denise Wilcox for a date.

Not that she'd ever asked.

No one—females in particular—had ever asked Dillon Cash for anything that didn't involve a hard drive or a motherboard. Not back in high school, when he'd been the all-state programming champion and not now that he owned the only computer repair shop in town. He'd never been a heartthrob. No women panting after him. No steady girlfriends. Not even a sex buddy.

Especially not a sex buddy.

No, the only girl who called him on a steady basis for something other than a quick computer fix was Meg, and she didn't really count because they were just friends.

Not that he was a virgin. He'd done the deed. Three times, as a matter of fact.

Three measly times in twenty-nine long years.

He definitely had much bigger problems than waking up with fangs.

He stared at his reflection again—the shiny hair, the vibrant eyes, the biceps, the hard-on.

A smile tugged at his lips.

Being a vampire definitely had its perks.

* * * * *

Dillon's story is coming,
but Cheryl Anne's getting hers first.
Don't miss the fireworks when Cheryl Anne
breaks loose in TEX APPEAL,
available in February,
wherever Harlequin Blaze books are sold

SPECIAL EDITION®

LIFE, LOVE AND FAMILY

*These contemporary romances will strike a
chord with you as heroines juggle life
and relationships on their way to true love.*

New York Times *bestselling author*
Linda Lael Miller
*brings you a BRAND-NEW contemporary story
featuring her fan-favorite McKettrick family.*

Meg McKettrick is surprised to be reunited with her
high school flame, Brad O'Ballivan. After enjoying
a career as a country-and-western singer, Brad aches
for a home and family .and seeing Meg again makes
him realize he still loves her. But their pride manages
to interfere with love…until an unexpected match-
maker gets involved.

*Turn the page for a sneak preview of
THE McKETTRICK WAY
by Linda Lael Miller
On sale November 20,
wherever books are sold.*

Brad shoved the truck into gear and drove to the bottom of the hill, where the road forked. Turn left, and he'd be home in five minutes. Turn right, and he was headed for Indian Rock.

He had no damn business going to Indian Rock.

He had nothing to say to Meg McKettrick, and if he never set eyes on the woman again, it would be two weeks too soon.

He turned right.

He couldn't have said why.

He just drove straight to the Dixie Dog Drive-In.

Back in the day, he and Meg used to meet at the Dixie Dog, by tacit agreement, when either of them had been away. It had been some kind of universe thing, purely intuitive.

Passing familiar landmarks, Brad told himself he ought to turn around. The old days were gone. Things had ended badly between him and Meg anyhow, and she wasn't going to be at the Dixie Dog.

He kept driving.

He rounded a bend, and there was the Dixie Dog. Its big neon sign, a giant hot dog, was all lit up and going through its corny sequence—first it was covered in red squiggles of light, meant to suggest ketchup, and then yellow, for mustard.

Brad pulled into one of the slots next to a speaker, rolled down the truck window and ordered.

A girl roller-skated out with the order about five minutes later.

When she wheeled up to the driver's window, smiling, her eyes went wide with recognition, and she dropped the tray with a clatter.

Silently Brad swore. Damn if he hadn't forgotten he was a famous country singer.

The girl, a skinny thing wearing too much eye makeup, immediately started to cry. "I'm sorry!" she sobbed, squatting to gather up the mess.

"It's okay," Brad answered quietly, leaning to look down at her, catching a glimpse of her plastic name tag. "It's okay, Mandy. No harm done."

"I'll get you another dog and a shake right away, Mr. O'Ballivan!"

"Mandy?"

She stared up at him pitifully, sniffling. Thanks to the copious tears, most of the goop on her eyes had slid south. "Yes?"

"When you go back inside could you not mention seeing me?"

"But you're Brad O'Ballivan!"

"Yeah," he answered, suppressing a sigh. "I know."

She rolled a little closer. "You wouldn't happen to have a picture you could autograph for me, would you?"

"Not with me," Brad answered.

"You could sign this napkin, though," Mandy said. "It's only got a little chocolate on the corner."

Brad took the paper napkin and her order pen, and scrawled his name. Handed both items back through the window.

She turned and whizzed back toward the side entrance to the Dixie Dog.

Brad waited, marveling that he hadn't considered incidents like this one before he'd decided to come back home. In retrospect, it seemed shortsighted, to say the least, but the truth was, he'd expected to be—Brad O'Ballivan.

Presently Mandy skated back out again, and this time she managed to hold on to the tray.

"I didn't tell a soul!" she whispered. "But Heather and Darlene *both* asked me why my mascara was all smeared." Efficiently she hooked the tray onto the bottom edge of the window.

Brad extended payment, but Mandy shook her head.

"The boss said it's on the house, since I dumped your first order on the ground."

He smiled. "Okay, then. Thanks."

Mandy retreated, and Brad was just reaching for the food when a bright red Blazer whipped into the space beside his. The driver's door sprang open, crashing into the metal speaker, and somebody got out in a hurry.

Something quickened inside Brad.

And in the next moment Meg McKettrick was standing practically on his running board, her blue eyes blazing.

Brad grinned. "I guess you're not over me after all," he said.

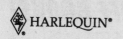

REQUEST YOUR FREE BOOKS!

2 FREE NOVELS PLUS 2 FREE GIFTS!

HARLEQUIN®

Blaze®

Red-hot reads!

HB07

HARLEQUIN®

Mediterranean NIGHTS™

*Experience glamour, elegance, mystery
and romance aboard the high seas....*

Coming in December 2007...

A PERFECT MARRIAGE?

by

Cindi Myers

Is there such a thing as a perfect marriage?

Trying to recapture the magic of their marriage
Katherine Stamos and her husband, Charles, take
a cruise aboard *Alexandra's Dream*. Once aboard
ship, it's still hard to leave their work behind and
much of what Katherine needs to hear remains
unsaid. Is it too late to find the excitement of love
after twenty years of marriage?

COMING NEXT MONTH

#363 A BLAZING LITTLE CHRISTMAS Jacquie D'Alessandro,
Joanne Rock, Kathleen O'Reilly
A sizzling Christmas anthology
When a freak snowstorm strands three couples at the Timberline Lodge for the
holidays, anything is possible...including incredible sex! Cozy up to these sizzling
Christmas stories that prove that a "blazing ever after" is the best gift of all....

#364 STROKES OF MIDNIGHT Hope Tarr
The Wrong Bed
When author Becky Stone's horoscope predicted that the New Year would bring her
great things, she never expected the first thing she'd experience would be *a great
one-night stand!* Or that her New Year's fling would last the whole year through....

#365 TALKING IN YOUR SLEEP... Samantha Hunter
*It's almost Christmas and all Rafe Moore can hear...is sexy whispering right in his
ear.* Next-door neighbor Joy Clarke is talking in her sleep and it's keeping Rafe up at
night. Rafe's ready to explore her whispered desires. Problem is, in the light of day,
Joy doesn't recall a thing!

#366 BABY, IT'S COLD OUTSIDE Cathy Yardley
And that's why Colin Reeves and Emily Stanfield head indoors—then it's sparks,
sensual heat and hot times ahead! But will their private holiday hometown reunion
last longer than forty-eight delicious hours in bed?

#367 THE BIG HEAT Jennifer LaBrecque
Big, Bad Bounty Hunters, Bk. 2
When Cade Stone agreed to keep an eye on smart-mouthed Sunny Templeton,
he figured it wouldn't be too hard. After all, all she'd done was try to take out a
politician. Who wouldn't do the same thing? Cade knew she wasn't a threat to jump
bail. Too bad he hadn't counted on her wanting to jump him....

#368 WHAT SHE *REALLY* WANTS FOR CHRISTMAS Debbi Rawlins
Million Dollar Secrets, Bk. 6
Liza Skinner, lottery winner wannabe, *thinks* she knows the kind of guy she should
be with, but is she ever wrong! Dr. Evan Gann is just the one to show her that a
buttoned-down type can have a wild side and still come through for her when she
needs him most....

www.eHarlequin.com

HBCNM1107